Two ...
One ***UNIFORMLY HOT!*** miniseries.

Harlequin Blaze's bestselling miniseries
continues with another year of irresistible soldiers
from all branches of the armed forces.

Don't miss

THE RISK-TAKER
by Kira Sinclair
January 2013

A SEAL'S SEDUCTION
by Tawny Weber
February 2013

A SEAL'S SURRENDER
by Tawny Weber
March 2013

THE RULE-BREAKER
by Rhonda Nelson
April 2013

Uniformly Hot!—
The Few. The Proud. The Sexy as Hell.

Available wherever Harlequin books are sold.

Dear Reader,

I had such a wonderful time writing *A SEAL's Surrender,* in part because I am the Queen of Goals, and the Soul of Stubborn. So I can relate to Cade Sullivan in a major way, because he is a man who believes in goals, too, and stubbornly refuses to give up on one—even after he's achieved it. But it was great, too, to explore Eden's challenges as someone who wants so much, and deserves so much—but isn't willing to actually ask for it. Oh, yeah, I can relate to that. Can you? I hope you'll drop me a note after you read the story and let me know.

And, as always, I love writing about the special fun that pets are. In this case, Jojo the goat, Mooch the mutt and Alfie the Yorkie—who is actually based on my mom's darling Yorkie. If you'd like to see Alfie, drop by my website at www.TawnyWeber.com and see his picture on *A SEAL's Surrender*'s page. And while you're there, I'd love it if you'd peek around, check out the recipes and contests. Or drop by Facebook and visit me at www.facebook.com/TawnyWeber.RomanceAuthor.

Enjoy!

Tawny Weber

A SEAL's Surrender

Tawny Weber

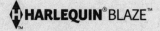

Recycling programs
for this product may
not exist in your area.

ISBN-13: 978-0-373-79743-1

A SEAL'S SURRENDER

Copyright © 2013 by Tawny Weber

This edition published by arrangement with Harlequin Books S.A.

For questions and comments about the quality of this book, please contact us at CustomerService@Harlequin.com.

® and TM are trademarks of Harlequin Enterprises Limited or its corporate affiliates. Trademarks indicated with ® are registered in the United States Patent and Trademark Office, the Canadian Trade Marks Office and in other countries.

Printed in U.S.A.

ABOUT THE AUTHOR

Tawny Weber has been writing sassy, sexy romances for Harlequin Blaze since her first book hit the shelves in 2007. A fan of Johnny Depp, cupcakes and color coordinating, Tawny spends a lot of her time shopping for cute shoes, scrapbooking and hanging out on Facebook. Come by and visit her on the web at www.tawnyweber.com.

Books by Tawny Weber

HARLEQUIN BLAZE

To get the inside scoop on Harlequin Blaze and its talented writers, be sure to check out blazeauthors.com.

Other titles by this author available in ebook format. Don't miss any of our special offers. Write to us at the following address for information on our newest releases.

Harlequin Reader Service
U.S.: 3010 Walden Ave., P.O. Box 1325, Buffalo, NY 14269
Canadian: P.O. Box 609, Fort Erie, Ont. L2A 5X3

With loving thanks to Anna Sugden,
simply for being awesome.

1

I WISH FOR A GUY who worships my body, is great at sex and makes me feel like a goddess. Someone who loves me, for me. Inside and out. And is really, really good at it.

And if he could be six foot two, with sandy blond hair and dreamy green eyes, a body that made nymphomaniacs weep and a smile that melted her panties, that'd be cool, too.

Eyes scrunched tight, Eden Gillespie let that visual play out for just a second. Then, with a deep breath, she opened her eyes wide and blew.

The flame went out. Thankfully. Because she'd blown so hard, the candle toppled from its perch on the chocolate cupcake. Good wishes did that, she told herself as she scooped up a fingerful of frosting and grinned at the woman sitting across from her.

"So? What'd you wish for?" Bev Lang leaned forward, her wild red curls bouncing like springs around her cheerful face.

"It's a secret. If I tell, it won't come true," Eden said primly before bursting into laughter. Yeah. Like she was gonna lose out on her body-worshipping lover because she put the word out that she was waiting? Still, she pulled her

cupcake closer and, since it was filled with molten chocolate, used a fork to enjoy the next bite…and fill her mouth
so she didn't blurt anything out.

Because you never knew with wishes.

"I can't believe you won't tell me. How long have we
been friends?" Bev asked, putting on her best 'affronted'
expression. It wasn't very effective since she still looked
like she was waiting for a white apron and her boyfriend,
Raggedy Andy.

"Eleven years?" Eden guessed, counting back to the
first day of high school. That'd been the year her dad had
died, leaving her mom too broke to keep paying the ex-
orbitant tuition to the private school Eden had always attended. Secretly terrified, Eden had put on a brave face in
hopes that the public school kids would accept her more
than the private school snobs had. Bev had been the new
girl in town, unaware that Eden wasn't acceptable because
of her zip code. By the time she'd learned the ins and outs
of Ocean Point social politics, she and Eden had been too
good of friends for it to matter.

"Then as your best friend since ninth grade, I figure it's
my job to help you with the wish," Bev decided, leaning
back in Eden's faded and frayed Queen Anne dining chair
and digging into her own cupcake. "I think this should be
your year for sex."

"An entire year, dedicated to sex?" Eden asked with
a laugh. She was sure there was nothing more than dust
motes and the faint air of neglect floating through the for-
mal dining room. But, still, it was all she could do not to
look over her head to see if the wish was written there in
the candle smoke.

"You should dedicate this year to the *pursuit* of sex."
Bev scrunched up her nose. "I don't want to hurt your feel-

ings or anything, but it might take a little effort on your part," she added.

When was the last time she'd had sex worth the effort? Definitely not with Kenny. Not with any guy, if she were being honest. Eden swirled her fork in the gooey rich chocolate, using it to make a design on the Meissen plate. After all, what better time for brutal self-truths than a girl's twenty-fifth birthday.

Kenny, the last guy she'd had sex with, had broken his foot trying to prove his manliness by doing it against a tree. Instead of accepting that he just wasn't he-man material, he'd blamed her.

No wonder her love life sucked. Look at what she had to work with.

"So I know why I should want good sex," Eden said, standing to clear their plates. "But why is my personal life on your radar?"

She didn't have to look to know Bev was following her to the kitchen. The rat-a-tat-tat of her high heels was a giveaway.

"Janie was in the shop yesterday," Bev said, sounding like her cupcake had been bitter lemon instead of rich chocolate. Bev owned Stylin', the best salon in town. And despite her penchant for wearing her own hair in rag doll fashion, she worked pure magic on everyone else. Enough magic to lure in the well-paying Oceanfront set.

"Ah." Eden didn't need to hear any more than that. She wasn't sure of the what, when and where, but she was sure she was the who the chatter had revolved around. That's how Janie and company worked. They wouldn't check in with Eden directly—they'd go to her best friend and mine for gossip.

"Don't let her get to you." Eden set the plates next to the sink.

"I'm just so tired of them talking about you," Bev grumbled, throwing the cupcake wrappers in the trash so hard that they bounced right back out. "They are all so snooty and rude, with their perfect lives bought and paid for by someone else."

"You think they have perfect sex, bought and paid for, too?" Eden asked, keeping her tone, and her expression, serious. She lost it, though, when Bev glared. Laughing, she asked, "What? You think I should get upset because they are talking about, let me guess… My love life, or lack thereof?"

"Well, it's not like they are saying nice things."

Eden shrugged, so used to pretending she didn't care that it pretty much came naturally to her now.

As if realizing she'd brought the bummer cloud to dim the party atmosphere, Bev clapped her hands together and exclaimed, "Presents! I'll be right back. I'm going to get your gift from the car."

Eden kept a cheery smile of anticipation on her face until the wooden screen door clapped shut behind her friend, then let it drop. She sighed, tossing the forks into the dishwasher and squirting liquid soap on a sponge.

Hot, happy sex.

Her chances of finding that were about as small and slender as the half-melted candle she'd just blown out.

What a waste of a wish.

She should have used it on her career.

Only out of veterinary school six months, she still had student loans and now a substantial mortgage on this house. It'd taken every bit of daughterly influence she had to convince her mother to let her buy it instead of putting it on the market. It'd also taken her entire savings account and the tiny trust fund left to her by her grandfather, but Eden loved her home and her heritage too much to see it sold to the highest bidder. And then there was the fact that there was enough property for her to set up her veterinary clinic.

With a shake of her head, she carefully dried the china and walked over to place it in the ornate cabinet with the reverence her great-great-great-gramma's plates deserved. Like most of the furnishings in her childhood home, the glass-fronted hutch was an antique. Rattling around here alone all the time, Eden sometimes felt like the house was just waiting for her to join the ranks of antiques so she'd better fit in.

It wasn't that she minded being alone, really. But like sex, sometimes a girl got tired of going it solo.

"The postman drove by when I was at my car," Bev said, returning to the room with a huge polka-dot box with a ribbon as curly as her hair. "I brought your mail in. Look, I think there are a couple of birthday cards here."

More because Bev was looking worried again than because of any curiosity to see who'd remembered her birthday, Eden took the stack of mail. Before she could get to the telltale bright envelopes, she noticed one from the bank. It was addressed to both her and her mother.

"What's up with this," she muttered, tossing the others on the counter and sliding her fingernail under the flap. She and her mother had no bank business together. And since Eleanor was tooling around the country, following the craft fairs in a new RV, Eden didn't hesitate to open the missive.

"What the…" She had to wait for the room to stop spinning and the buzzing to clear from her ears before she could read the letter again.

Nope. The words hadn't changed.

"I'm going to kill her," she muttered through gritted teeth.

"What? Who? Where's a shovel so I can help you bury the evidence."

"My mother took out a loan against the house." Fury pounded at her temples like a gorilla with a sledgehammer. Knowing the words wouldn't change, no matter how many times she glared at them, Eden crumpled the letter in her fist and threw it against the wall.

"I thought the house was yours," Bev said quietly. "I thought you bought it from her."

"My cousin Arnie is a lawyer. He wrote up a legal document that said the house was mine once I took over the mortgage, and then added my name to the title. But he'd advised against transferring it out of my mom's name at that point because I was still carrying student loans and needed the bank to approve another so I could start a new business."

But why hadn't he checked for loans against the property when he'd changed the title?

"She didn't warn you? Talk it over with you before taking out the loan? Give you a heads-up that you were about to get hit with a big ole bill? Nothing?"

"Warn me? She didn't even call to wish me a happy birthday," Eden said, her laugh only a little bitter, wishing she could be as shocked as Bev. "To her credit, she probably forgot."

"About the loan?" Bev scoffed, her freckled face furrowed in fury.

"About my birthday."

And how sad was it that the fact that her mother forgot her birthday hurt more than a bill for thirty grand. Eden reached for the phone, then curled her fingers into her palm. As much as she wanted an explanation, an assurance that the payment-in-full had been mailed to the bank, she knew better.

Eleanor Gillespie didn't worry about little things like money. She was too flaky to let the mundane rain on her creative lifestyle.

Glancing at the bank's letter, Eden cringed. Flake or not, her mother had made a mess of things. And, as usual, Eden was the one who had to figure out how to clean it up. Because if she didn't find some money quickly, she could lose the house. The property that'd been in her family for five generations. Her home, her place of business.

Her life.

As if reading her mind, Bev asked, "What are you going to do?"

Eden blinked fast to clear the dampness from her eyes. What she *wasn't* going to do was cry, dammit.

"I guess I'm going to find thirty thousand dollars." Where on earth was she going to find that on top of her other debts? And why hadn't her mother arranged for a repayment plan? Coming up with that kind of money in one fell swoop was close to impossible. Eden rubbed her fingers against the sudden pounding in her temple, then walked over to retrieve the letter. She'd have to study it, contact the bank, so she understood all the details.

"You're really going to take on your mother's loan?"

"It's against my property. I have to take it on. At least, until she turns up again and deals with it herself. But she's tooling across the country from craft fair to art show right now. I have no idea when I'll hear from her. Or when she'll come home and clean up her mess."

"How are you going to get the money?"

Hell if she knew.

Every penny she earned was earmarked. Despite her fancy address, she was living a ramen noodle lifestyle here.

There was nothing of value to sell. Oh, sure, she still had her great-grandma's china and there were a few antiques left floating around. But they were all she had left of her family. Well, those and her mother. And right now she was pretty sure the china was worth more.

Eden took a deep breath. There had to be a way through this. She just had to think. *Think, Eden.*

Her eyes fell on a square envelope embossed with ivy and roses. The monthly garden club meeting. She wrinkled her nose, wondering if they resented having to send her the invitation as much as she hated getting it.

Because she was the last person the socially upstanding ladies wanted invading their exclusive get-togethers. But the Gillespie name guaranteed her an invitation.

"The Oceanfront set," she exclaimed, snapping her fingers.

"What was the question again?" Bev asked with a confused look.

"I'll hit up the country club ladies."

"For loans?"

Eden cringed. Handouts? Oh hell, no. She was nobody's charity case.

"For clients. They are all big on their designer pets. I just have to get two, maybe three of them to start using my veterinary services, and more will follow."

"How much are you going to charge?" Bev asked, her eyes huge with a horrified sort of glee.

Eden laughed.

"Just enough that they consider the services exclusive. All it will take is a few of them using me as their vet, a little behind the scenes hype and pretty soon I'll have a well-heeled clientele. I might not be able to pay off the entire loan at once, but if I can get enough of a down payment and show the bank that I have the potential income, I'll bet I can swing a deal."

Maybe.

And maybe was all she needed.

Eden reached for the phone again, quickly dialing the head of the Garden Club.

Five minutes and three grimaces later, she hung up with a triumphant smile.

"Why'd you RSVP for two?" Bev asked, pulling her head out of the pantry to give Eden a suspicious look.

"Because you're going with me."

"Oh, no," Bev declared, emptying an armload of bins and jars onto the chipped tile counter. "I'm not a member. They won't let me in."

"You're my guest."

"They aren't going to want me there," Bev predicted.

"They don't want me there, either." Eden shrugged. "They'll just have to deal with us. Because I need you with me."

"For moral support?"

Eden wasn't sure how much good moral support would be when faced with forcing a tight-knit group of women to accept an outsider at one of their chichi meetings. But she did need someone to play off. Someone who could talk up her veterinary skills and give her the verbal setups she'd need to spike home her point if this plan was going to work.

"What are you doing?" Eden asked, eying the eggs and butter that had just joined the flour, brown sugar and peanut butter.

"This is clearly a cookie situation," Bev said, digging a bag of chocolate morsels out of the freezer.

Before Eden could decide if the two of them eating what, if the butter and eggs were anything to go by, would be a double batch of peanut butter chocolate chip cookies was a good idea, there was a rumbling outside.

Company? Or another birthday surprise? Maybe her mother had found a way to send the plague by UPS.

Or, Eden squinted, in a shiny new Jaguar.

"Hey, cool. It's like the birthday fairy heard your wish," Bev joked, joining Eden at the door to see who was pulling up the weather-pitted driveway.

Recognizing the car, Eden frowned.

Even though they were neighbors, Robert Sullivan never visited.

So the only way the birthday fairy was playing into this particular arrival was if his son, Cade, had hijacked the Jag and was driving up to make all of Eden's fantasies come true.

Cade Sullivan.

Tall, blond and gorgeous, with hypnotic green eyes and more charm than a proud momma's bracelet.

The sexiest guy to ever set foot in Ocean Point.

High school quarterback. Class president. Navy SEAL.

Her hero.

She knew most people in town who didn't have membership with the exclusive Ocean Point Country Club—and even a few who did—saw Robert Sullivan as a major asshole. But when she looked at him, all she saw was an older version of Cade. The guy who always rescued her from mishaps, who'd never made a tag-a-long girl five years his junior feel stupid.

The guy she'd had a crush on since she was seven. The one she'd spied on at the small, private lake that bordered their two properties. The man who'd formed her every basis for what spelled sexy in a guy.

Eden sighed.

Then Robert's car swerved.

Eden gasped.

The Jaguar made a beeline for the faded brick arch that welcomed people to the Gillespie house.

Eden hit the door running. Just as she made it to the

bottom of the steps, the car slid into the unyielding bricks
with a sick crunch of crumpling metal.

"What's happened? Who is it?" Bev called as Eden
sprinted across the lawn, skidding on the gravel driveway
in her hurry to reach the car.

"Call an ambulance. Tell them to hurry." Eden stared at
the older, colder version of her favorite fantasy, her breath
tight in her chest. She checked the pulse at his throat to
be sure, then gave a shaky sigh. "Robert's hurt. I think he
might have had a heart attack."

IT WAS LIKE WATCHING a bunch of virgins tour a whorehouse.
Lieutenant Commander Cade Sullivan shook his head at
the current crew of Basic Underwater Demolition SEAL
trainees slogging through the wet sand, each carrying a
dripping log over his shoulder.

"Were we ever that green?" he wondered aloud.

"You weren't," Captain Seth Borden said with a laugh,
clapping Cade on the back. "You were one of the most
focused BUDS we've seen come through here. I've been
a MTS a long time, but even I can't always tell which
guys will make it through Hell Week. Sometimes none
do. But when you came through, every instructor knew
you'd graduate."

Borden was a Master Training Specialist. One of the top
at Coronado's Naval Special Warfare Center, as a matter
of fact. He was a machine. A guy who'd dedicated thirty
years to the navy and scared the hell out of most people.

Cade considered him a crusty old bastard who drank
like the sailor he was, cussed with flare and played a
wicked hand of poker. And when they weren't in uniform
or on base, he was Cade's favorite uncle.

"Why'd you haul me down here?" Cade asked, grimacing when one guy tripped over his own feet, taking three

others down with him and sending his log flying ahead into the back of two more. "Wanted to make sure I appreciate how good my team is?"

He grinned when three wannabe SEALs sidestepped the downfall and just kept on going. Those guys, they had what it took.

"You need a reminder?"

"Nope." Cade's smile faded. He knew damned well that he served with some of the best SEALs in existence. Guys who gave their all, like his buddy Phil Hawkins, who'd given it right to the end. A familiar band of grief tightened in Cade's chest, as it did whenever he thought of the loss. The Three Amigos, Phil, Cade and Blake Landon had gone through BUDS together, had served in the same platoon, on countless missions together. They embraced everything that being a SEAL stood for. Brotherhood. Dedication. Excellence.

And now the Three Amigos were two.

"C'mon in. We'll have a cup of coffee."

Grateful for any distraction from the gnawing emptiness that had started to overshadow his SEAL career, Cade followed the captain to his office. He shook his head when Borden held up the coffeepot. While on tour, he might have to stick with field rations, but the rest of the time, he opted for quality. From the looks of that pot, the sludge in the carafe was barely digestible.

"So?" Cade prodded, knowing he didn't need to repeat the question.

"You're coming up on your PRD."

Cade wasn't surprised at the captain's statement. Borden figured he'd recruited Cade to the SEALs. Since being a SEAL had been Cade's goal from the time he was twelve, he didn't think recruiting was the right term, but he let the old man have his illusions.

"Not for six months," Cade said, referring to his Projected Rotation Date, the time when he'd be up for reassignment. He'd been based here in California for eight years. Chances of being sent to Virginia or Hawaii were slim, but possible. Maybe a transfer was a good thing, though. He could start fresh, get away from the constant reminders of his lost friend. "Why?"

"I want you to consider taking your MTS cert."

Cade laughed and shook his head. "Why the hell would I want to be certified as a trainer?"

"You're a freefall jumpmaster, took gold in the Excellence in Pistol Shot, and were awarded the Silver Star. You aced out of Sniper School. And then there's the advanced counterterrorism technology training. You're one of the elite. You got the goods, boy."

Cade rocked back on the heels of his jump boots and grinned. Yeah. That was a pretty sweet list of qualifications. He'd worked damned hard, and loved every second of getting all of them. But all he said was, "So?"

"So we could use you here. The certification, a year as a trainer—it'd bump your pay grade and move you a lot closer to those captain's bars."

Cade frowned. He didn't care about the pay or rank. But he did care about losing his edge, about this depthless funk he'd sunk into, dragging his team down, too. He glanced out the window at the grown men falling all over themselves in the surf, struggling like toddlers to reach their boats. Those guys wanted to excel. To be the best. And he could be damned good at helping them get there. But to do that, he'd have to quit being a SEAL. And he didn't quit. Not one damned thing.

So he shook his head. "Nah. I'm good."

"Don't you think it'd be mighty impressive?" the captain asked as he and his steaming cup of coffee settled behind the desk.

"Borden, I'm already a SEAL. There's not a damned thing more impressive than that."

"Sure, maybe to the ladies."

"Who else matters?" Cade laughed.

Hell, it was rare that he ever even had to pull out the SEAL card to impress a woman. He looked good enough that the women tended to fall all over him anyway. They always had. And it wasn't ego talking. He credited genetics for his sandy blond hair, sharp green eyes and chiseled features and the navy for his ripped body.

He had nothing to prove to anyone else.

"You want to climb higher than Lieutenant Commander?"

Cade shrugged again. Rank and money didn't mean anything to him. Neither one had the thrill, the excitement, or the rock-solid satisfaction of being a part of Special Ops. At least, up until last fall, when Hawkins had taken a piece of shrapnel to the head while under Cade's command.

"I'll bet there are some people who'd like to see you move up the ranks," Seth said, staring into his cup like it held some fascinating secret. Or, more likely, because he didn't want his expression to give away his trump card.

"I don't live my life for other people," Cade countered with a grin, dropping to a chair and getting ready to play. Mind games were almost as much fun to win as war games.

"What about Robert?"

Cade's smile fell away.

"I definitely don't live my life for my old man."

"Not saying you should. But I'll bet it'd go a long way toward keeping him off your back for a while."

"You mean it'll keep him off your back?"

Robert Sullivan had married Seth's little sister Laura

thirty-five years ago and had probably muttered an average of a few dozen words a year to his brother-in-law since the reception. Less after they'd lost her to cancer five summers ago. But Robert somehow managed to find a few here and there to touch base with Seth for a little secondhand haranguing for his one and only child.

"Robert doesn't bother me," Cade's uncle said, dismissing him with a jerk of one shoulder. As if his ex-in-law was that easy to flick off.

Cade wished that were so. But he knew better. Robert Sullivan, of Sullivan Enterprises, specialized in tenacity, had the personality of a bulldog and the charm of a cactus. He'd been furious when Cade had joined the navy instead of taking his rightful place at the helm of the family's financial consulting firm.

"If he doesn't bother you, then why are you using him as bait?" Cade challenged.

"Because you're a damned good soldier. A fine SEAL and a strong leader. I don't want to see you derailed. You're on edge lately. That's the kind of thing that some people look for, try to take advantage of in order to make things go their way," he said, referring to Cade's father. "A break would let you figure it all out, before you're played."

His pleasant expression didn't change, nor did his body shift even an inch as a painful sort of tension spiked through Cade's system.

"No offense, Captain," Cade said with a grin as he got to his feet. "But I don't give a good damn what my father does. And nobody plays me. Not even the old man."

To Robert Sullivan, Cade was a pawn. A useful tool. He'd expected his only child to follow in his footsteps, to learn the ins and outs of finance and take over the vast Sullivan holdings if and when Robert deemed it time.

Cade had never been interested in any of that. Not even

as a kid. So he'd never let the old man in on his plans. He'd enlisted the day he'd turned eighteen, three months before he'd finished high school. Already knowing the value of good strategy, he'd waited to tell his father until the morning after graduation. And he'd left for basic training right after the ensuing big ugly fight.

It wasn't just that he didn't want to take some bullshit business major if his father covered tuition that made him decide not to go to college.

He simply hadn't wanted to wait to get started in the navy.

And then, like now, he hadn't given a damn about rank.

He just wanted to be a SEAL.

He was born for the military.

He just had to remember that and get through this damned... What did his squadmate and amigo, Blake's fiancée, Alexia, call it? Journey of grief. Stupid thing to call being pissed off over losing his buddy. And definitely not something he wanted to talk about. Not to Blake, not to Alexia. And definitely not to his uncle.

Before he could make excuses to leave, Cade's cellphone rang.

"Speak of the devil," he muttered, noting the number on the screen.

"The old man?"

"Close enough—it's my grandmother."

The only thing that kept Cade from turning his back on his family, and all the drama and crap that went along with it, was his grandmother. He would do anything, even play nice at holidays, to make Catherine Sullivan happy.

With that in mind, he gestured his apology to Borden and took the call. Five minutes later, he wished he hadn't.

"Robert had a heart attack," Cade murmured as he slid the phone into his pocket.

"Is he okay?" Seth asked, looking up from the paperwork he'd been pretending to do to give his nephew some semblance of privacy.

"He's in intensive care. They don't know if he's going to make it."

Seth frowned, coming around the desk. "Are *you* okay?"

Cade shrugged. He didn't know what he was. Numb. Despite a lousy, contentious relationship, shouldn't he care that his father might die? That he was hanging by a thread?

Cade's mind couldn't quite take it in.

He was a SEAL, specially trained in multiple ways to cause death. He'd served during wartime. He'd watched men die. He'd held one of his best friends as life drained away. It wasn't that he wasn't familiar with the concept.

But his father? He'd always figured the old man was too stubborn, too obnoxious, too uncompromising to allow it to happen on anything but his own approved timetable.

"You need anything?"

Cade gave Seth a blank look, then shook his head. "Gotta see my CO, get leave. Grandma wants me home."

Seth's wince pretty much summed up Cade's lifelong feelings about returning to the Sullivan Estate.

Cade grimaced in return. "Looks like I'm getting that break after all."

2

"DID YOU HEAR? Cade Sullivan is back."

Eden shook her head as twitters and giggles filled the room, women from the ages of eighteen to sixty-eight offering up a communal sigh. From what she'd seen, the members of the Garden Club rarely agreed on anything. Leave it to Cade Sullivan to bring women together.

But as hot and sexy as Cade was, he wasn't the kind of stud she wanted to talk about right now.

It wasn't like she wasn't a fan of Cade herself. She adored the guy. Heck, she'd love to *do* the guy. But she was here to talk up her business. To try and garner a few new clients. Instead, the entire conversation had been derailed by the homecoming of the town hero.

Cade was good at that kind of thing. Making women sigh, fantasize, and if rumors were true, have some mighty fine orgasms. At least, that's what the Cade-ettes, as those lucky few who were in the know liked to call themselves, claimed.

"I heard he's here for a month. He doesn't come back often, does he?" Bev mused, her eyes dreamy. No doubt visualizing Cade in some form of undress. "It's been, what? Ten years since he left?"

"Twelve," Eden corrected absently, leaning over to scoop up a bite of her friend's lemon chiffon cake. The fork halfway to her mouth, she noticed all the stares aimed her way and shrugged. "It's not like I'm marking off the years in my diary. He left for the navy the same week I broke my foot the first time. He's the one who carried me home from the lake."

"Did you know him well?" asked a pretty blonde whose name Eden didn't remember. The girl had married her way into the Ocean Point high society, so she didn't have firsthand knowledge of the almost mythical wonderfulness that was Cade Sullivan.

"Oh, please," Janie Truman scoffed, sliding into an empty seat at the table and taking a single grape from the bowl in the center. "You barely knew Cade Sullivan. Sure, he rescued you a few dozen times. But that's sort of what he does for a living, isn't it? You were like basic training."

Her laugh was too bubbly for Eden to take offense. At least, not unless she wanted to look like a bitch. That was the problem with Janie. She always came across as all smiles and charm, even while she slid her pretty jeweled knife between your ribs.

Eden sighed, wondering why belonging to this group was her holy grail. The ugly was always as subtle, but as real, as the expensive perfume. But only to outsiders, she figured. The only way to avoid being the butt of their jokes and pitying looks was to belong.

"I'd say growing up next door to the Sullivans means she probably knows Cade well enough," Bev defended, her irritation on Eden's behalf shining bright.

"Sort of," Eden demurred, not sure she wanted to share just how much about Cade she did know. Instead she settled on the simple facts. "Cade's five years older than I am, so we weren't in school together, didn't run in the same crowds. Cade was busy with football and the swim team and I was playing with animals and volunteering at the shelter."

How was that for an opening to talk about veterinary care, Eden thought, giving herself a mental back-pat.

"Captain of the football team. Class president, homecoming king," Janie rhapsodized, her sharp chin on her hand as she gave a dreamy sigh, ignoring any references that included Eden. "Oh, to be a Cade-ette…"

"Cade-ette?" Bev asked with a laugh. She gave Eden an *are you kidding* look.

Eden grinned. It was a little shameless, as far as titles went. Still, it carried as much cachet as an Oscar did for an actor. "It's silly. When Cade was in high school—"

"Junior high, even," Janie interrupted.

"Maybe," Eden acknowledged, wrinkling her nose. "That's awfully young, though. Not for Cade, of course, but for the girls? But nobody knows for sure, do they?"

"Knows what?" Bev prompted before Janie could launch into one of her typical attempts to prove that she did, indeed, know everything.

"Knows when it all started, what the rules are or even who's in the club," Eden said. "The story goes that Cade, while being quite the ladies' man even in his teens, knew he wanted out of Mendocino County and wasn't about to let anything—not even a girlfriend—keep him here. So while he played the field, he kept things simple, uncomplicated."

"In other words, he was really careful about sleeping around because he didn't want to be trapped. Not just because he's super cute, but because the Sullivans are filthy rich," Janie explained, eyeing the cake with an envious look before nibbling on another grape.

"But after a while, girls started bragging. I think the allure of having done Cade Sullivan was better than a pair of diamond studs, and they just couldn't keep from showing off." Eden remembered the almost mythical shot to fame the girls would get, being fawned over, buddied up to, romanced by other guys. "Pretty soon, the Cade-ettes had an even more exclusive membership than the country club."

"Exclusive, and elusive," Janie interrupted. "There weren't many who could make that claim to fame. Maybe a dozen at the most."

"How do you know they were telling the truth?" Bev wondered. "I mean, if he was determined not to get trapped, would he really sleep around, even with a dozen girls in four years?"

"Sixteen years," Janie corrected. "That dozen counts the girls he was with before—and after—he left for the navy."

"You mean the club still has openings?" Bev joked.

I wish, Eden almost said aloud. Horrified, she focused on shoveling cake into her mouth to keep it busy. She had a bad habit of looking before she leapt, and speaking before she thought. Usually, she didn't worry about the results. But this was Cade they were talking about. And she cared about everything that had to do with Cade Sullivan.

Which was why she'd never shared, not even with her best friend, how often she'd seen Cade at the lake behind their properties. Skinny dipping sometimes, practicing martial arts others. But usually with a girl. Eden had rarely seen the girl's face, but could see through the bushes clearly enough to know they both usually ended up naked.

He'd been gorgeous, even as a teen, with the body of one of the Greek Gods Eden had been fascinated with. Tan, sculpted and, well, huge, he'd been worth the many bouts of poison oak she'd gotten spying through the trees.

She dropped her fork onto the empty plate and reached for her iced tea, needing to cool off.

"So this rumor, you believe it?" Bev prompted.

"Sure." Eden shrugged. "I mean, the few who did try to claim they'd done Cade Sullivan were outed as liars pretty fast. Nobody but the Cade-ettes themselves know what the secret is that proves the truth. I guess they think it's a pretty good secret, too. Like I said, it's been twelve years since he left and they still aren't talking."

And while she'd only watched him a couple of times before embarrassment and a heart-crushing envy had made her avoid the lake altogether just in case he was there, she'd never seen any distinguishing marks or heard him use any special phrases that might stand out as tells.

"Everyone wanted to be a Cade-ette," Janie said with a sigh, either forgetting her constant diet as she scooped up a fingerful of chocolate from the cake in front of her, or envy making her so morose that she didn't care.

"Everyone?" Bev asked, her eyes questioning Eden.

Eden just shrugged again. She wasn't going to lie to her best friend, but neither did she see any point in admitting that she would have given anything to join the well-sexed crowd. But not for the title. Nope, she just wanted Cade.

"Ladies, time to get to work," Gloria Bell, the Garden Club president called, clapping her hands for attention. "The Spring Fling is just around the corner. Our biggest society ball needs the best flower arrangements, don't you think? Come on now, chop chop."

Most of the older women got up and gathered around the three head tables, discussing what kind of flowers screamed fancy party. That left Eden and a dozen women her own age seated next to the dessert buffet. A fact that seemed to pain half of them, since they studiously kept their gazes averted. Eden, who while carrying a plethora of issues and challenges, could happily eat anything and everything without gaining an ounce, just grinned.

This was the only way she stood out, a wren among

peacocks. They were grace, she was clumsy. They were as beautiful as money could buy, she was as average as broke could maintain.

"I can't believe nobody has shared the secret yet. Are you sure there is one?" Bev asked, wrinkling her nose. "I mean, it sounds like more of an urban legend than fact, you know?"

"Oh, it's real." Crystal Parker leaned forward, her eyes shifting to the matriarchs to see that her mother was occupied before she shared in a low tone, "My sister, Chloe, was almost one of the Cade-ettes."

"Almost?" gaped Bev. "How is one almost in the club?"

"She went on a few dates with Cade the winter before he graduated. The two of them were getting really friendly, if you know what I mean, during the high school Winter Bash and Chloe got a little loud. Then the principal, Mrs. Pince, walked in on them. Chloe said Cade charmed his way out of a lecture, but never did ask her out again."

She gave a good-humored roll of her eyes, as if her sister's getting busted making out still amused her.

"Of course, that couldn't have been as embarrassing as what happened to poor Eden here," Janie said with a giggle before patting Eden's hand. As if that friendly gesture made the joke any easier to take. "You never have told us the real story about what you and Kenny Phillips were really doing when he broke his foot and ended up covered in a nasty rash."

Eden pressed her lips together in a grimacey sort of smile, hoping someone, *anyone,* would change the subject. She didn't need anyone speculating about what particular sexual position Kenny had been in when he'd fallen.

Cade had rescued her then, too. Turning the tables nicely, he'd shown up at the lake to find her with his best buddy from high school. The poor guy had been rolling around naked in a patch of poison oak while clutching his broken ankle.

"Girls," Gloria called, gliding over like an elegant steamship. "Chitchat is over. Now it's time for work."

"I can help," Eden offered, gratefully getting to her feet. But in her desire to escape further sexual comparisons, her hip bumped the table, sending the unlit candles toppling, forks bouncing off plates and the grapes rolling over white damask to the floor.

"Oh, well…" Mrs. Bell grimaced, then shook her head. "Thank you, dear. But we need someone with a little better eye for color. Janie, why don't you and the girls come along now and see what you think of the plans."

En masse, all of the women except Bev and Eden migrated to the front of the room. To the popular section.

Eden sighed, pushing aside the last plate of dessert, this one a double-chocolate brownie.

"What's wrong? It's not like you to stop rubbing your super-fast metabolism in the princesses' faces before you've tried every dessert," Bev said quietly.

Although Eden noticed a few envious glances at three empty plates in front of her, all she could focus on was the giggling group of women all bundled together around the flower displays. All fitting in, all contributing meaningfully. All perfect, even if they couldn't eat more than two hundred calories at a time.

"Nothing. I'm just tired," she excused, not completely lying. She was tired.

Tired of being so easily dismissed.

Tired of feeling like a failure.

Tired of wallowing in mediocrity.

Just once, she wanted to be admired. To stand out—in a good way. To feel like someone special. To be part of the in-crowd.

And maybe she should wish for a time machine, too, and blast back to high school when she should have gotten over these silly issues.

"Oh, Eden," Lilly-Ann Winters, who sat at the next table, called, offering a charming smile. "I'm so glad you made it to the meeting this month. You so rarely do."

"I usually work Thursday afternoons," Eden said with a cautioning look toward Bev. Lilly-Ann had a trio of Parti Yorkies and a pedigree Persian at home.

"Oh, you still have that, um, job?" Lilly-Ann asked, a rapid flutter of her lashes probably supposed to be a distraction from her having no clue what Eden did.

"I opened my veterinary clinic six months ago, and yes, it's still in business," Eden said with a nod, amping up her smile and getting ready to pitch her real reason for subjugating herself to this torture. "You should bring Snowball in for a checkup. I have a wonderful new program for cats, an all-natural diet and supplements that are guaranteed to add luster to her coat."

"Oh, no. Snowball only sees Dr. Turner," Lilly-Ann said, her eyes wide with horror at the idea of taking her precious Persian anywhere but the most expensive vet in three counties.

"I understand," Eden said, pulling out the diplomacy she'd been practicing since she'd called in her RSVP. "Dr. Turner has a wonderful reputation. And he's so popular. Just last week someone was saying she had to wait a month to get her puppies in for a routine exam."

Lilly-Ann's smile tightened at the corners. Bingo. Eden knew the only thing the other woman hated more than designer knockoffs was having to wait for *anything.*

"Don't you worry about emergencies, though?" Eden continued, leaning forward and speaking in a hushed, let's-share-a-secret tone. "You can't take risks with a feline as delicate as Snowball. If you wanted to just bring her by for a checkup, I'd have her information on file in case, God forbid, there was ever a crisis."

For one brief, gratifying second, Lilly-Ann looked tempted. Then she gave Eden a once-over, as if to remind herself who she was dealing with, and shook her head. "No, no. Thanks, though. Dr. Turner has a pet ambulance. I'm sure we'll be fine."

With that and a giggling little finger wave, she got to her feet. Bev stood, too, an argument obviously on her lips.

Eden shook her head, gesturing to her friend to sit. What was the point? She needed clients desperately. She'd hoped a few of the women would, if only for faux-friendship's sake, give her a chance. But to them, and to most of Ocean Point, she'd always be the klutzy girl who'd broken Kenny's foot while having sex. A joke. An average, broke joke who was about to lose her home. Because she'd tried everything she could think of, even calling her mother—who hadn't answered—to find a way out of this financial mess. If she didn't come up with the money—or at least enough to negotiate a deal—within three weeks, her home, her heritage, would be gone.

"Brownie?" Bev offered again with a sympathetic frown.

Eden shook her head.

Some things, even chocolate couldn't help.

SHE WAS STILL ASKING herself what the point of it all was two hours later as she drove home.

"Well that was a total waste of a Saturday," Bev declared from the passenger seat, nibbling on the piece of cake she hadn't let herself eat in front of the other women. "I can't believe that in a roomful of thirty women, twenty-six of them have pets."

"And of that twenty-six, I couldn't get a single client," Eden mumbled, wishing she hadn't wasted Bev's time. "Still, it wasn't all bad."

She didn't have to take her eyes off the road to know Bev had shot her an incredulous look. Probably a sneer, too, if Eden knew her friend.

"Hey, I made contacts. That counts. They might not have signed on board today, but all it takes is one good word, one rich matron with a colicky dog, and I'm set." She slanted a sideways glance toward the passenger seat. "And, hey, at least dessert was good."

"Well, I'll give you the desserts point. But do you really think a matron or two using you as their vet is going to stop the bank from calling in the loan?" Bev didn't even bother with the skeptical look this time. Her tone, even wrapped around chocolate icing, spoke volumes.

"Until I come up with something better, this is the best shot I've got," Eden said morosely.

Damn her mother. Damn *herself* for not forcing Eleanor to sign herself off the property when Eden had bought her out. She should have known better. According to her personal bio, Eleanor Gillespie was a free spirit. A wild wind that couldn't be tamed. Eden sighed, her fingers clenching and unclenching on the steering wheel. A loving flake who specialized in making life difficult for her only child.

From preschool when she'd used all of Eden's classmates to test her politically incorrect, factually accurate and visually scarring nursery rhymes to high school when she'd volunteered as a parental chaperone at the senior all-nighter, then lectured everyone on birth control, sexual satisfaction and the benefits of a vegan lifestyle, she'd been a challenge. But she was also fun and bubbly, creative and clever, and loved Eden in her own self-absorbed, offbeat way.

Eden rounded the corner of narrow country road, tall trees looming on either side of the asphalt. But just as she passed the pretty stone gates that led to the Sullivan Estate, something white flashed. She lifted her foot off the gas, peering through the window. She saw it again.

White fur and gray spots.

She slammed on the breaks.

Bev's hand shot forward, bracing against the dash.

"What the hell…?"

Half on and half off the road, Eden killed the car engine and threw her door open.

"It's Paisley," she called as she hurried around the car toward the stately bank of large maple trees Laura Sullivan had planted when she was a young bride. "Mrs. Carmichael has been frantic since the cat ran away last week. We need to rescue her."

"That cat is evil," Bev muttered, following her. "Besides, do you really think *ran away* is the right term? That sounds so innocent. I heard it was more like a prison break, complete with injuries and property damage."

Eden waved that away. So Paisley was a little difficult. She was a rare snow Savannah. Being standoffish was a characteristic of the breed, as was the need for play and fun. Since Mrs. Carmichael wasn't much good at either, the poor cat had probably run off out of boredom.

Before she could explain the psychological makeup of Savannahs, there was a loud screech, then a crash boomed out from behind the women.

Except for a teeth-clenching wince, Eden froze.

Bev screamed.

Cringing, they both pivoted toward the car.

Eden had forgotten to set the parking brake.

She and Bev stared at the tree-hugging vehicle in silence.

Damn.

"This is a bad week for cars around you," Bev observed with a resigned sort of huff.

Eden groaned. It was like she was a walking, talking accident waiting to happen.

The car wasn't new, or even in very good condition, but it'd been big enough for her to transport anything smaller than a horse, was paid for and had looked decent enough not to irritate wealthy potential clients.

Now the passenger fender had formed an intimate relationship with a redwood.

After staring at the car for a solid minute, Eden sighed and deliberately turned her back on it to walk the rest of the way across the street.

"Aren't you going to do something? Where are you going?" Bev hurried after her. When Eden stopped under a tree and peered through the leaves, then reached up to test the strength of one branch, the cheery blonde gaped. "You can't be serious? You're still going to try to rescue the cat?"

"Why not? The car is already a mess—I might as well have something to show for it." A safe, secured pet was a reasonable price to exchange for a molested fender. And maybe, if she was lucky, this could be her chance to bond with Paisley and get in Mrs. Carmichael's good graces.

"Paisley," Eden called in a cajoling tone. The cat, perched high on a maple branch, stopped its upward bounce to toss Eden a disdainful look. "C'mere, pretty kitty."

"Why don't we just call Mrs. Carmichael and tell her we saw her cat. She can come get it herself," Bev suggested when her stilettos slid on the dirt bank. "And give us a ride while she's at it."

"Sure, a sixty-year-old woman needs to be climbing a tree after her cat," Eden dismissed, her own stubby-heeled

Mary Janes not slipping at all—girls who tended to trip over their own feet wore stilettos at great risk—as she made her way around the base of the maple.

After a few more calls, a few snarky remarks from Bev and another dismissive look from the cat, Eden sighed. She looked up the road, then down, to make sure no cars were coming. She only climbed trees once in a blue moon, but somehow she always managed to get busted.

"You're lookout," she told Bev. She glanced down at her pretty blue cotton dress, then tugged the back of the pleated skirt forward between her thighs, tucking it into the wide black belt. "There, modesty intact."

"There, fashion destroyed," Bev said, shaking her head in dismay. "If anyone asks, I tried to talk you out of this. I pointed out the likelihood of you falling, of you breaking yet another bone or something horrible happening to your hair."

Eden's fingers combed through the thick swath of heavy brown hair at her shoulders and gave Bev a confused look. "My hair?"

"I think it's the only thing you haven't messed up so far. It's due."

Eden grimaced, then shrugged. Bev was probably right. Some people might lament their fate, others would spend hours in therapy. She figured that by simply accepting that she was a little accident prone, she was not only ahead of the game in terms of dealing with emergencies—because after all, she created at least one a month—but she was saving a fortune on psychiatric fees.

"Watch for cars," she warned again, reaching up to grab the closest branch.

"What do I do if I see one? Whistle? Throw myself across the driver's window to hide their view?"

There might be a few drawbacks to having a BFF with

a smart mouth, Eden decided as she levered her body onto
the first branch.

"Just give me enough warning so I can hide," she said
as she gained her balance and slowly stood upright to reach
for another limb.

With Bev's voice droning in the background, covering
everything from the fact that she'd never learned to climb
a tree to the insanity of grown women acting like squir-
rels, Eden scurried higher.

A minute later, she was one branch away from Paisley.

"Hi, sweet kitty," she said in a soft singsong voice. "Are
you up here playing Queen of the Jungle? You should be—
you look like royalty."

She kept the soothing tone going, her outstretched fingers in constant motion to get the cat's attention.

It worked. After a few seconds and a cautious sniff, the
exotic white cat was nudging her broad forehead against
Eden's knuckles.

"Oh, aren't you sweet."

Unable to resist, Eden gave herself a moment to cuddle
and pet the pretty cat before tucking her under one arm
and slowly lowering herself until her butt met the branch.
Like scooting down a rickety ladder, she went one branch
at a time, with plenty of cuddling in between. Finally she
was close enough to hand the cat to Bev.

"Why don't you put her in the car," Eden instructed, her
belly flat against a wide limb that was about six feet from
the ground. "Crack the windows, and there's a bottle of
water and portable pet dish in the trunk. If you'll sit with
her, she'll probably drink a little."

Despite her earlier opinion that the cat might be evil,
Bev didn't hesitate to reach out and cuddle the gray-spot-
ted feline. Paisley gave a meow of protest, and threw an
injured look toward Eden, but didn't try to escape. Eden

waited until her friend and the cat were safely inside the car, treats and water dispensed, before she lowered herself to the next branch.

There. She smiled her relief. Almost down.

It was the smile that did it, she figured.

Because she went from enjoying an easy descent to being suddenly trapped in the space of a heartbeat. Like an anchor, something held tight, so she couldn't move.

Breathless, Eden twisted to see what was wrong.

Then scowled when she saw that the strap of her shoe was caught on a branch. Eden tugged. The shoe stuck. She tried to slip it off, but the branch was too rough, scratching painfully against the soft flesh of her instep.

A minute later she added cursing to the mix.

"Haven't we been here before?" a husky voice asked.

Oh, hell. Eden froze. She hadn't even heard a car. Please, oh, please, let him be talking to someone else.

"That is Eden up there, right?" the voice asked.

Double hell.

She shook her head, hoping the move would shift the curtain of hair from blocking her view.

Her heart, already pounding like a freight train, sped up. What little was left of her breath escaped her lungs in a rush.

She twisted her torso, angling herself sideways to make sure the face matched the voice.

Gorgeous green eyes, a tanned complexion over sculpted cheekbones and a strong jawline. Wide, full lips stretched in a smile that bordered on laughter. And the sexiest man-dimple she'd ever seen.

Her eyes widened and she gave a long, lusty sigh.

Didn't it just figure? At least she'd tucked her skirt in so she wasn't flashing him. Sure, she might have a few dozen fantasies about sharing her undies with this particular man. But this position wasn't featured in a single one.

So she did what she always did when caught in an uncomfortable situation.

She smiled and made the best of it.

"Hi, Cade."

3

"Do you do these things just to keep me in practice?" Cade asked, grinning at his favorite perpetual-victim, her silky brown hair a dark curtain over a face he knew would be sliding into a sheepish smile.

Eden Gillespie always looked sheepish when she had to be rescued. Something, if he'd ever considered it, he'd have figured she'd have outgrown. He eyed her legs, smooth and bare all the way to the top of her hot-pink panties thanks to the way her dress was hanging. Her arms were wrapped around the tree limb and one foot dangled while the other was caught in a snarl of branches and leaves. Clearly he'd have figured wrong.

"Consider it my welcome-home present," she muttered, blowing a puff of air so her hair cleared enough that he could see the resigned amusement in her big brown eyes.

That was one of the things he'd always admired about Eden. She could laugh at herself. So many of the girls he'd grown up with, and the women he'd dated for that matter, took themselves and life way too seriously. They were so worried about controlling the impression they made, they didn't let themselves just live.

Without thinking, his eyes shifted back to Eden's legs.

Long and sleek, they wrapped around that big, hard branch. He frowned at the scrapes and faint reddening of her tender flesh, for the first time ever tempted to kiss away a boo-boo. All the way up to her panties. Practical cotton, he noted, his mouth going dry, but in a fun, sassy color. Since she was facedown on the branch, the curve of her butt was perfectly highlighted in that pink fabric. His fingers itched to touch, to see if her curves were as firm as they looked.

Whoa. Not cool, he lectured himself. Lusting after the sweet girl next door was walking an awfully close line to settling down. Nothing wrong with it in the big picture, but in his personal rulebook? Totally out of the question.

"Want some help?" he offered, wondering how many times now he'd had to hurry these rescues along because of a hit of inappropriate lust. After all, he was pretty sure he'd been hauling her out of scrapes since his pre-teen days. But it'd only been since *that* rescue, when he'd seen her naked, that the sight of her made him instantly horny. He sighed with relief. There, now he was only a standard guy, not a weird pervert with a superhero complex.

"I can do it," she muttered, tugging her foot to try and loosen it from the branch. Her shoe, a cute little black strappy thing, was good and stuck. She sighed and slanted him a rueful look. "But maybe you could just unhook my shoe for me?"

Cade didn't bother arguing. He reached up and pulled the twigs from her foot. Then he wrapped both hands around her surprisingly narrow waist, easily lifting her from the overhead branch. It was like doing a military press, he thought with a grin as he lowered her body toward the ground.

Except he hadn't counted on her shocked reaction. She gasped, struggling a little as if wanting him to let her go. Since he wasn't about to drop her three feet to the ground, he shifted. Her breasts skimmed his chin. He froze. Other than to gasp and grab on to his shoulders for support, so did she.

Cade had felt the same energy pounding through his body when he held a live grenade. Danger, excitement, all senses on full alert.

Wrong, his brain screamed. Eden was the sweet girl next door. The same girl he'd been rescuing for years. She wasn't supposed to inspire this degree of lust. The kind that made him want to take her, right there against the tree. He didn't care that they'd only said a dozen or so words to each other in years, or that her friend was over there, face pressed against the window of the wrecked car, watching.

It was neither of those things that had Cade ignoring the hot need in his belly, or his body's demand that he taste her, touch her.

It was the flutter of Eden's lashes. The way her pulse trembled in her throat. The tiny trembles of her fingers where they dug into his shoulders. He, and his wicked desires, were out of her league.

So, nope. Not giving in to the need.

But that didn't mean he couldn't enjoy himself up to that limit line.

Grinning, he slowly brought his arms down. He didn't let go of his hold on her waist, so her body had to slide, in one long glorious trip, down his.

His eyes never left hers. There was something heady, intense, in seeing the heat flare, then her gaze blur with passion.

As soon as her feet hit the ground, she pushed away like he was fire, too hot for her to touch.

"Thanks again," she said as she stepped backward. Her foot caught on a root and would have sent her sprawling if he hadn't grabbed her.

"Babe, I live for these moments," he told her in a husky tone, only half-teasing. Because he really did. Eden always made coming home fun.

"Me, too."

The look on her face, a mix of horror and chagrin, said loud and clear that she had, as usual, spoke without thinking.

He should let her off the hook.

It wasn't like he was going to give in to the heat between them. Ever since his first romp at the tender age of fourteen, he'd made it a point to stay relationship-free and keep his sexual encounters easygoing and simple. There was nothing simple or easygoing about Eden.

Except looking at her. That was as simple and easy as breathing. And talking to her. He'd never had any hesitation there. Listening to her laugh was pure pleasure.

Hell.

"C'mon, I'll give you a ride home," he said, his words a little gruffer than he'd intended.

"I can get home."

Cade didn't bother arguing. He just pointed to her fender, wrapped around that tree as intimately as he'd like to see Eden wrapped around his body.

"Oh. Yeah." She sighed, looking from the fender to her friend, then to Cade. Her gaze shifted again to the cat, then his car. Finally she shrugged. "Thanks. We appreciate the ride."

As soon as both women—and the feline—were settled in his borrowed BMW—the quiet redhead in the back and Eden and her rescue cat in the front—he started the car.

"So, you still seeing Kenny Phillips?" he asked, hoping like hell she'd say yes.

"Not anymore." She did that cute little nose-wrinkling

thing then shook her head. "He never quite forgave me for breaking his foot."

It'd been Kenny's screams that'd caught Cade's attention a couple years back, leading him to rescue a stunning, naked Eden. Cade was still baffled by that situation, since Kenny was nothing if not a missionary kind of guy. How the hell did a guy break his foot having standard, missionary sex? You'd think it'd take a swing, a tube of body lube and a few leather straps to reach that level of risk.

"I don't think you lost out on much. Dating is a full-contact sport," he told her with a laugh.

Unlike a lot of women, Eden didn't get that speculative, *how interested are you in playing the game with me* look in her eyes. Instead she just shrugged.

"I guess Kenny decided to sign up for a lower-risk league, then," she informed him as she rolled her ankle first one way, then the other. "And he took most of his teammates in town with him."

"Wimps," Cade muttered. What kind of jerks blamed the girl for their own incompetence? Sure, Eden was a little accident prone. But she was sweet and sexy in that girl-next-door way. She was fun and easy to talk to, and unlike so many others around town, she didn't play the user game. A guy would be lucky to date her. If he was interested in dating, that is.

"So you're saying you wouldn't be scared?" Eden challenged. Her chin was high and her tone light, but he could see the vulnerability in those gold-flecked brown eyes.

"Sweetie, unless a woman straps an explosive device around her waist and insists we go dancing, there's not much that will scare me." Cade laughed.

"So you'd date a girl who had a reputation for being a little clumsy?" she asked quietly.

Well, how the hell had he missed that trap? Cade

frowned, even as a gurgle of horrified laughter came from the backseat.

"I don't base my dating choices on things like that," he sidestepped. Then, to further cement the *keep out* message, he added, "Really, I don't see myself dating at all in the next little while. Between the old man in ICU and my grandmother needing me, I figure I'll be pretty tied up until I return to base. Gramma said something about some deals my father was trying to wind up when he had the heart attack, something with important timing. I'm probably going to have to take care of that, too."

Ah, silence.

He had no idea what'd caused it, but he'd take the stilted quiet over tap dancing around a verbal trap any day. Other than the uncomfortable shifting her friend did in the backseat, nobody made a sound. Even the cat quit purring.

Still, by the time they reached Eden's place, less than a mile up the road, tension tight enough to bounce coins off rippled across the back of Cade's neck. He drove down the long, circular driveway, his discomfort slowly fading as he noted how rundown the Gillespie place had become. The immediate yard around the huge house was still tidy, but beyond the fence, weeds were brushing the trees. Even the once vivid white paint on the shutters was graying, chipped and curling.

One of the outbuildings looked like the roof had collapsed and someone—probably Eden—had built a crude wire fence to pen up a goat and what looked like a horse-size dog.

"Thanks for the rescue. And the ride," Eden said when he stopped in front of wide bank of steps leading to her front door.

"Anytime," he told her. "Just try to keep your accidents

scheduled for my visits home. I hate to think of you hanging from a tree and only wimps here to save you."

She laughed, the pained discomfort chased away by amusement. "Would you believe that I usually manage to rescue myself when you're not around?"

Cade considered that for a second.

Then he shook his head. "Nope."

Her cheeks warm with a pretty pink wash, Eden gave him a sweet look from under her lashes. The kind of look that should make him feel protective. Or manly, like a superhero.

Not horny like a sailor on leave.

Time to go, he decided.

Leaning one elbow on the seat, he angled himself around.

"It was nice to meet you," he told the quiet redhead in the backseat. She gave him a wide-eyed, about-to-hyperventilate look.

Because he was a SEAL, trained in multiple ways to kill men and defend his country? Or because of his high school rep and near rock-star dating status?

Then the redhead blushed.

Yep. Rock star.

"Cade?"

He looked at Eden with a friendly smile, ready to politely brush off her thanks.

She was staring at the cat on her lap, as if one glance away would send it leaping out the window.

"Did you maybe want to get drinks with me? Sort of a welcome-home and thank-you combination?"

Drinks? Unless that meant standing in line together to each buy their own bottle of water at the corner market, drinks were a really bad idea. Drinks were code word for tiptoeing into dating territory. A precursor to, part of or windup from something more intimate.

A huge mistake.

It wasn't that Cade didn't date. And he was nowhere near being a monk. But here in his hometown, the rules were different. Here, the women tended to see him as Robert Sullivan's son. The guy who'd get the key to the Sullivan coffers. A great catch.

Not that women didn't have an agenda outside of Ocean Point, as well, but usually that had more to do with being able to say they'd been with a SEAL. Being a notch on a woman's lipstick case, he was okay with. Being the target of her engagement ring search, he wasn't.

Still, this was Eden. He'd need to let her down easy.

"Sure," he heard himself say instead. "A drink sounds good."

His momentary chagrin at giving in to the urge fled quickly at the look of surprise on Eden's face and the delighted shock on her friend's.

She'd expected him to say no. To be a wimp.

Her friend had figured the same, hopefully without the wimp part. He knew his rep, and the status-obsessed focus of a lot of the country club set that Eden ran with. The Sullivans were big shit around town. The Gillespies barely danced around the fringe. From the time he was fourteen, he'd heard hundreds of lectures on dating, all focused on the girl's last name, never her first. God, he hated that. That, and the way everyone always gossiped, judging each other's worth by who they dated or the limit on their credit card. Hell, before he hit the end of the driveway, he'd bet her friend would have texted twenty of her best friends to tell them the news.

Within ten minutes, forty more people would probably have texted her back with varying degrees of shock, denial and outright horror at the idea of a Sullivan lowering himself to date a woman like Eden. One who lived in a rundown house, whose sexual encounters resulted in broken bones and who wrecked cars to rescue cats.

Who didn't date for status.

Who liked him for him, not because of his last name.

Who made him feel like the hero she always teased him about being.

Any intention Cade had of retracting his agreement disappeared. He was going out for that drink, and he was going to make damned sure that Eden—and anyone else who might be curious—knew he was glad to spend time with her.

"Tomorrow night?" she asked, her casual tone at odds with the tension in her eyes.

"Six okay?"

She gave a tiny frown, her arched brows drawing together for a second before she nodded. Then she leaned down to grab her purse, gathered the cat closer and reached for the door handle.

"Let me," Cade offered. Giving in to rare mischief, he grinned, then leaned across Eden's body to open the passenger door from the inside. He let his forearm brush, ever-so-lightly, across her breasts. She gave a tiny gasp, her doe-eyes rounding with shock. Her scent wrapped around him, earthy and sweet at the same time, like honeysuckle at midnight.

He forgot about the woman in the backseat, ignored the purring mass of fur draped across Eden's lap. All he cared about was the woman staring up at him like he'd hung the moon, lit the stars and made the sun rise when he whistled.

Without thinking, he leaned down and brushed a whisper-soft kiss over her shocked mouth.

"Thanks for the welcome home," he murmured, immediately leaning back. He kept his expression light. Amused even. As if his own body hadn't just gone into overdrive at the taste of her lips under his.

"Anytime," she murmured, draping the huge cat over her shoulder and sliding from the car as if in a fog. He waited until her friend was out, too, then shifted the car into gear.

A quick glance in the rearview mirror confirmed that both women were still staring.

Cade grinned.

Maybe the next couple of weeks wouldn't be so bad after all.

THERE WAS NO WAY in hell he was sticking around another couple of weeks. Cade clenched his teeth to keep the fury inside, both because spewing it would upset his grandmother, and more to the point, because he refused to let his father know he was pushing buttons.

"You need to step it up, put in more effort," his father lectured from the crisp white sheets of his hospital bed. A chorus of beeps and buzzes accompanied his rant, medical equipment proving that a man could have a heart and still be a heartless bastard. "You've been doing the same thing for years now. When are you going to get a promotion? What's it take to get a raise in that military you serve? Don't my tax dollars pay enough for you to make a little more? Call up your ambition, boy. Push harder."

It didn't stop there. Cade made a show of inspecting his boots while Robert droned on.

And on and on.

And on.

It was like he was trying to spew out every demand, every put-down he could as fast as possible because he knew the drugs and his body's need to heal would soon take over and knock him back out.

Cade wished they'd hurry the hell up.

At first, he'd listened in sympathy to the slurred words dragged down by drugs and age. He'd stared at the man lying in the hospital bed, trying to reconcile the sagging gray skin and fragile appearance with his no-bullshit father. Seeing him tapped every which way into wires and machines, for the first time in his life, Cade had felt sympathy for his old man.

Once Robert had awakened, that sympathy had lasted about five minutes.

Now, an hour later, Cade was once again asking himself if his mother, rest her soul, had bumped her head a few times before agreeing to marry such a tyrant. He'd served under some hard-asses in his years, had worked with egomaniacs and assholes. But none held a candle to his old man.

"You hear me, boy?"

"I'm not the one under medical observation," Cade said laconically, rocking back on the heels of his boots and giving his father the easygoing smile he knew irritated him the most. "My hearing is just fine."

The older man's eyes, just as green as Cade's though blurred now, narrowed.

"I wasn't sure. You're always being shot at, or surrounded with bombs going off all around you. You might have lost a few brain cells."

Cade's smile slipped a little. Nope. All he'd lost was one of his best friends. But Robert Sullivan wouldn't give a damn about that.

Hell, the loss of his wife had only slowed him down a few weeks. If he missed her now, Sullivan-the-elder never showed it. Cade wished, for the first time in his life, that he had a little of that distance, that he could tap into that emotional void and just not care. Not feel the pain. Not carry the almost too heavy to bear weight of responsibility.

Gut clenched, he stared at the tubes pumping health into his father, focusing on the slender plastic until he could slam the lid shut on the gnawing pain.

"I've got to say, I find it difficult to believe you haven't made Commander yet. You clearly aren't applying yourself. You want me to die here, knowing my son quit for nothing? That he walked away from his familial obligations to play soldier and then didn't get anywhere?"

Cade's fists clenched and his blood boiled. He took a step forward, not caring that he was teetering on the edge of an explosion.

"Robert."

That's all it took. One word from Catherine to settle her son against his well-fluffed pillow. And, more likely her goal, to make her grandson stand down without challenging his father's obnoxious remarks.

Cade hated that the old man got to him. He didn't have a damned thing to prove to anyone. Still, he couldn't shake the tension knotting his shoulders or the fury coiling in the pit of his belly. Why had he come back? Why wouldn't his grandmother let him fly her to San Diego once in a while, or at least listen to his oft-repeated advice that she give up on that crazy illusion that they were a cozy family.

He needed to get out of here. And, if he was smart, he should go call Eden and cancel drinks. A night of thinking had provided plenty of reasons why it was a really bad idea. Mostly because all the images he'd had involved stripping those pink cotton panties off her.

"I'll be back to pick you up in a couple hours," he told his grandmother.

Catherine patted his hand with her own gnarled one,

her expression peaceful, even with the tiny line of worry creasing her brow when she gazed at her only child. It must be a mother thing, Cade thought, shaking his head. That ability to see something positive where nobody else could.

"I have a job you need to do," his father called out when Cade's hand closed on the doorknob. "I loaned one of the neighbors some money with their property as collateral. Turns out they took out a loan with the bank, too. If the bank decides to foreclose, I've got no leverage to get my money back. So I need you to collect before that happens."

Since there were only two tracts of land close enough to be considered neighbors, and one belonged to Cade's grandmother, that meant Robert was talking about the Gillespie property.

Cade was surprised his fist didn't crush the knob.

With the same caution, vigilance and care he'd take in facing an armed enemy, Cade slowly turned around.

"I'm not available for side jobs," he said, keeping his tone light, his expression neutral. Both because he didn't want to upset his grandmother, and yes, because he knew it'd piss his father off even more. Petty, he acknowledged, given that the guy was in a hospital bed. But he couldn't help himself.

"You need to do this one. If you don't the bank is going to take the property. I'll lose my money, and the Gillespie girl will lose her home."

"Eden borrowed money from you?"

"Eleanor did."

Robert didn't meet the shocked looks of his son or his mother. Looking frail again, he glared at the tubes in his hand for a second, then muttered, "She kept trying to sell me those ceramic things she makes. Erotic art, she calls it. I finally gave her the loan against the house just to get her to go away. Now she's off, who knows where, and not paying her debts. Figures."

Cade should be amused that someone could knock his father down a peg or two. But he was too busy worrying about the sweet girl next door.

"Eden has no idea?"

"As flaky as Eleanor is, I doubt it. I was on my way to tell Eden she was going to have to make good on her mother's debt when all of this…" he waved his tube-tapped hand toward the machines "…happened. I've been a little preoccupied since."

"You'd take the home out from under a girl you watched grow up. A neighbor? She made you cookies," Cade said, gesturing to the tray on the sideboard with a bright red bow and get-well card.

"The bank's the one that would be taking it out from under her. I just want to collect on what's due to me," Robert argued, shifting to his elbow to glare at his son. "Eleanor shouldn't have taken that loan if she couldn't pay it off. That's on her, not me."

"You're the one trying to kick Eden out of her home."

"The bank's going to kick her out. I'm the one stuck in this damned hospital bed peeing into a hose while I get screwed out of ten grand."

Maybe there was justice in the world.

It was something Cade had believed, once. Just like he'd believed he could make a difference. Now, he didn't have much faith in anything.

He couldn't stop his father from being a jerk, from hurting people. But he'd be damned if he'd help him.

But if he walked away, what happened to Eden? Cade remembered the state of the property. Run-down, rough looking. She didn't have the money for upkeep, which meant she probably didn't have enough to pay off his father. Or the bank.

He wanted to say screw it all. To get the hell out of here and go back to San Diego. For the first time since Phil had died, Cade wanted a mission. Something dangerous and intense. Something with a lot of guns, escalating violence and hopefully a shot at a little hand-to-hand combat.

"Cade," Catherine said, her quiet voice still loud enough to be heard over the sudden beeps and buzzing of the machines monitoring Robert. "That sweet girl is going to need help. Someone has to step in and keep the bank, and others, from taking her property. You'll take care of this for her until Eleanor gets back to pay her debts, won't you?"

Like a plug had been pulled on his fury, Cade sighed.

What was it about his grandmother? She never raised her voice, never said a harsh word. Yet nobody could say no to her. Including him.

"Sure, yeah, I'll take care of things," he promised quietly.

What else could he do? It was Eden. He couldn't, wouldn't, let her be tossed out of her house. It was the only home she'd ever known. Hell, until her mother had taken up mobile living, it was the only home the last four generations of her family had ever known.

He had to find a way to save it. To save her.

And, maybe, just maybe thinking of her as a mission, as a personal responsibility, would keep his hands off her sexy ass.

4

"Is this too modest?"

Eden turned one way, then the other, trying to see how she looked. Her bureau mirror only showed the top two-thirds of her body, though. So she couldn't tell if the borrowed skirt was sexy, slutty or simply stupid.

"Shouldn't you be asking if it's too revealing? Or," Bev leaned her head sideways and squinted, "if you should be wearing underwear?"

Eden clapped both hands on her butt cheeks, checking to make sure they weren't hanging out. The skirt wasn't that short, was it? After assuring herself it hit mid-thigh, she glared at her friend.

"Just because it doesn't leave panty lines doesn't mean a thong isn't underwear," she chided. And she wasn't about to ruin the look of her cute little black skirt with panty lines. Short, but not so much that she'd be in danger of flashing her goods, it fit like a glove, and showed off the benefits of being able to eat anything and everything and not gain an ounce. Her black blouse billowed, making her feel like a sexy poet with its wide ruffles and full sleeves.

Not a bad *just drinks, not really a date, but don't you wish it were* look, she decided. She leaned closer to the mirror to check her makeup. Smoky but subtle, like the magazines suggested. Glistening pink on her lips, just a hint of shimmer on her cheekbones and an extra coat of mascara.

She looked like herself, but not.

Exactly what she'd been hoping for.

This was it. Her chance to make one of her favorite fantasies come true. To make Cade Sullivan see her as more than a rescue operation, a charity case. A cute pet he needed to pull from the occasional tree.

"So?" she asked again, giving Bev an expectant look.

"You look great," the other woman said, sitting cross-legged on Eden's bed wearing blue jeans and a frown.

The bedroom, like the rest of the house, was a little worn. The last time the paint had been refreshed, Eden had been thirteen and going through her Grateful Dead phase. Thankfully, the years had faded the virulent purple to a smoky amethyst. Evening light, soft and gentle, wafted through the open windows, bringing with it the occasional bark from the barn. Eden had three dogs kenneled in what she affectionately called her veterinary hospital, but what most everyone else called a wreck. She'd spent the afternoon giving them, the horse and the goat extra play time and exercise to make up for the fact that she wouldn't be down to visit later. Because, please-oh-please fingers crossed tight, it'd be too late when she got home.

"This is the first time I've ever actually spent any time with Cade. He actually seems like a nice guy," Bev said, her tone implying he was pure poison. "Are you sure you want to go out with him?"

Trying to figure out what to do with her hair, because hanging flat was so boring, it took Eden a few seconds to take that in.

"What? You think I should only go out with guys who aren't nice?"

"No. But you have to admit, you don't have very good dating luck. Or should I say, the guys who date you don't have very good luck."

Which inevitably resulted in Eden not getting lucky. But that was beside the point. Or maybe it was the point, she frowned. Something to consider if tonight didn't work out. Maybe she should learn not to maim her dates or something.

"Cade's a navy SEAL. I'm sure he's been trained to handle dangerous situations," she said drily.

"Maybe," Bev allowed with a grimace. "Still, I don't think this is a good idea."

"Okay, what're you so worried about?" Eden asked with a sigh. When a friend brought over her entire collection of makeup, clothes and shoes for you to choose from, a girl was somewhat obligated to listen to her concerns.

"Nothing, just, well, you know how the women were talking yesterday. This guy's got such a reputation that they give out groupie insignia for being with him. Is that really the kind of guy you want to date?"

Hell, yeah.

Eden managed to keep the exclamation to herself, though. She didn't think it'd allay Bev's worries to hear her rhapsodize about how great it would be to finally be considered a part of the "in" crowd. To be worthy of an insignia, or even talked about in any way that didn't invoke pitying eye rolls. God, she hated the eye rolls.

"It's fine," she said instead. "Cade's just a friend and this is just a welcome-home, thanks-for-hauling-me-out-of-the-tree drink. Nothing more."

"He kissed you."

Eden's entire body went hot.

The memory of his lips, so soft yet firm, as they'd brushed hers had kept her awake half the night. His scent, rich and earthy, had wrapped around her. If she closed her eyes and imagined, she could smell him again. Still…

"That wasn't a kiss. That was just a peck, a friendly gesture. A real kiss requires tongue," Eden replied. Although she was pretty sure Cade could take her from tepid to boiling with just his lips.

Rumor supported her theory, as did the peeks she'd taken at his lakeside rendezvous. Cade Sullivan was the sexual bomb. She was sure of it. And she wanted, more than anything else, for him to make her explode.

"Look," she said, going for distraction before her blushes gave away how much she really wanted Cade, "I'm just having drinks with him. It's a good thing and it will help me out of the jam I'm in."

At Bev's quizzical look, Eden continued. "You know what the bank manager said. Because my mother took out that loan against the house while it was still in just her name, and because we just added my name to the title instead of transferring it when I took over the mortgage, I'm stuck. Cousin Arnie is sure Mom meant to pay that off. I'm sure she meant to pay it off. And as soon as I reach her, I'm sure she'll take care of it. But in the meantime, I need to make those payments."

"So?"

"So… People will see us, get to talking, and you know how the gossip chain is in this town. Everyone wants the inside scoop but doesn't want to look like a snoop. So they'll try to be casual, make appointments for me to see their pets. Or their mom's pet, or their neighbor's pet, whatever they can get." Eden wrinkled her nose, equally amused and irritated. "I'll get some new business, put the money toward a reasonable payment to the bank and buy some time until I can reach Mom."

Every word was true. Except that not one of them had anything to do with why she wanted to go out with Cade.

"You're using this guy to build your business?" Bev asked, her face all screwed up with distaste.

Eden paused in the act of twisting her hair this way, then that, to stare at Bev in the mirror. She made it sound so bad. Like Eden was one of those girls in the club, only after Cade's status. They didn't care if they dated him, or his father, as long as the last name was Sullivan. She wasn't like that.

She opened her mouth to explain that to Bev, then closed it right back up. Because explaining would require she give her real reason for wanting this date so badly.

She wanted to seduce Cade Sullivan.

She wanted to strip him naked, drive him crazy and make him wild for her. To become a memory that he could think about on those nights before a scary mission and smile. To stop being the cute, accident-prone girl next door in his mind and become the sexiest experience he'd ever had.

She wanted to experience wild, intensely fabulous sex. To find out if all those rumors about his prowess were real. She wanted to be a Cade-ette, even if nobody but she and Cade knew it.

She wasn't using Cade Sullivan for his name or connections or to better her social standing, dammit.

She was using him for his body.

But Bev wouldn't understand that. She was too much a romantic. And also just a little bit of a worrywart. The minute she knew what Eden was planning, she'd try to talk her out of it.

Eden pressed one hand to her stomach, trying to soothe

the dancing butterflies, and figured she wasn't in any position to defend her decision.

"It's just drinks," she finally said. "How much using can be done over a beer?"

"You don't drink beer."

"Cade does."

Eden huffed at Bev's narrow look. "So I know what he drinks. You drink rum and cola. Janie drinks cosmopolitans, Crystal likes lemonade spritzers and Mrs. Winters chugs Kahlúa. What's the big deal?"

"How do you know these things?" Bev asked, sounding amazed as she finally relaxed enough to come over and start helping Eden fix her hair.

"I usually end up on bartender duty at the Spring Fling," she said, shrugging as if not ever being asked out on a date since the broken foot fiasco didn't bother her.

"Oh." Bev didn't say another word. A deep frown etched on her face, she did some twisty fun thing with a few braids, a flip here and a tuck there and turned Eden's heavy blanket of usually blah hair into a kicky style.

"Wow." Eden twisted one way, then the other, her grin getting bigger with each turn. "This is so cool. It's casual, sexy but still me. How do you do that?"

"I keep telling you, I'm good." Bev stepped back and peered through slitted eyes at the style, then shrugged. "If you'd let me do more than give you a trim, you'd find out. You could totally rock a shorter style. Something sassy."

"I don't think I'm the sassy type," Eden admitted. Although she was doing a pretty good impression right now. Cute top, with just a hint of sheer to show her red bra. Sexy skirt, just tight enough to remind her to sit like a lady so as not to show off her thong. And killer shoes. She eyed the black pumps with their red soles and white polka dots and wondered how many steps she'd make in them before she twisted something.

"You know, there are other shoes that would go with the outfit. Flats would work."

Eden grinned at the worry in Bev's voice. Geez, a few minor twisted ankles, a broken bone here and there and a girl got such a rep.

"I'll be fine. Since you're giving me a ride into town, I don't have to drive in them. I'll only have to walk from the car to the club, and back again."

Eden would have rather driven herself, but with her car at the Larkin's Body Shop, her only transportation at the moment was a ten-speed bicycle.

"Why isn't Cade picking you up?"

"He called earlier to change the time and mentioned that he's at ICU visiting his dad. I figured it'd be easier to meet him in town instead of making him drive here, then back there."

"So it really isn't a date," Bev said with a relieved sigh.

"Nope. Just two friends getting together for a welcome-home drink."

And, if Eden had her way, it would mark the beginning of a very hot, very sexy, very intense, and more importantly, very short affair.

AN HOUR LATER, Eden walked into the Oceanside Bar like a pageant queen on a slick catwalk—with slow, careful steps and pure concentration. What had she been thinking, suggesting they meet for drinks here?

"Eden?"

Ignoring the shocked looks, she called her hellos, but didn't slow down. If she did, she'd have to get the walking momentum going again, and that might not happen.

She should have hit the liquor store and invited Cade

over to her place. It'd be less nerve-racking to try and seduce a guy in private, wouldn't it? Of course, then he could leave as soon as he'd accepted her welcome, thanks and cold brew.

Eden's foot slipped, her ankle taking a sharp left while her foot went to the right. Damn. She quickly regained balance, hoping nobody had noticed, then hurried her mincing steps to the bar's entrance and its lovely carpeted floors. Bev had been right. Flats would have been much smarter.

"Eden?" This greeting didn't carry that air of shocked amusement. Nope, Cade's voice was filled with pure, masculine appreciation.

And he looked just as good as he sounded. Dark jeans, a forest green button-up shirt and a charming smile made him the sexiest guy in the room. Of course, she was pretty sure he could have been wearing fatigues or grease-stained coveralls or nothing at all and still have taken the sexiest title.

Oh. Nothing at all. She gave herself one second to enjoy that image, then stepped forward to join him.

"Hi," she greeted with a smile, reaching out to give his forearm a quick rub.

"I'm sorry I'm late—there was a dog emergency. Not the medical kind, but the howling kind. I wasn't sure if your grandmother was staying at the Wayfarers Inn to be close to your dad, but just in case she'd gone home, I wanted to make sure it was quiet for her. So, you know, I had to settle them. The dogs," she finished painfully.

Staring into Cade's wide eyes, she watched him try to process her babbling. Well. There you go. She hadn't fallen on her butt, but had managed to make an ass of herself anyway.

She wanted to groan. She was supposed to be sexy. Seductive, even. She'd have turned on her exceptionally high heels and walked right back out of the room, except that, well, yeah, the heels were exceptionally high. And Cade did look really good...

Too good to walk away from after just one strike.

"Okay, then," he said with a laugh. "I've got us a table already. Let's have a seat and you can run that by me one more time."

She glanced toward the dimly lit, secluded tables at the back. But they were all taken. Eden did a quick survey of the ocean-facing deck, looking for an unclaimed spot there. Nothing.

"Right over here," Cade said, gesturing toward the first-date section. The not-sure-you-want-to-see-it-through seating area. Where there were plenty of people-watching opportunities to distract from boring conversations, no hint of romantic potential and easy access to all escape routes.

Well.

Her inner seductress wanted to huff herself into a pout, then crawl into a corner. But Eden was too practical for that. She'd invited Cade out for a "welcome home, thank you for rescuing me from the tree" drink. He didn't know he was about to be seduced.

Yet.

So she followed his gesture, swaying a little more than usual thanks to the high, high heels, and made her way through the questioning looks and outright shock to their very public table.

Maybe the skirt was a little shorter than she'd realized? When Cade held out her chair, she glanced over her shoulder to offer a smile of thanks as she gratefully—if not gracefully—slid into it. And saw the look in his eyes.

Smoldering hot.

Thigh-clenchingly intense.

The kind of look a guy offered just before he stripped a girl naked.

Her breath caught tight in her chest. Eden wasn't sure what to do, what to say. She wanted to turn the rest of the way around, wrap her hands around his shoulders and climb up his long, hard body. She wanted to shift upward just a little, and try out that kiss from yesterday again. But this time with tongue.

She wanted to make him wish he'd gotten one of those dark, secluded booths, dammit.

Before she could give in to any of that temptation, he straightened. She had to force herself not to whimper when he moved away to round the table.

Then he sat down.

The look in his eyes was gone, as if it'd never existed. Instead, his gaze straddled the line between neutral and friendly. Like, now that he'd thought about seeing her naked, it just wasn't that interesting.

"Hey, Eden, I didn't know you were the buddy Cade was meeting," the waitress said, stepping over with a friendly smile for both of them. "What can I get you?"

Buddy? Eden, her teeth hurting from being clenched so tight, debated. She could be obvious and order a Screaming Orgasm or a Suck, Bang, Blow. Or try for sophisticated and order a glass of Chablis from the Naked Winery.

After a second, though, she sighed and went for the old standby. "A pomegranate margarita, blended. Thanks."

"Another beer," Cade added, lifting his bottle. As soon as the waitress left, he gave Eden one of those friendly, distant sort of smiles that she was sadly used to here at the Wayfarers. But never from him.

Despite the heat she'd have publically sworn was flaming between them the day before, he was suddenly acting like he barely knew her. What happened to treating her like she was a cute kid? Or his personal rescue victim. Neither role was one Eden particularly cared for—especially since neither one would get her into his pants any time soon. But they were better than being treated like a vague acquaintance from back in the day.

Determined, calling up the same stubborn focus she'd used to put herself through veterinary school, to build a business from the ground up in her hometown, in order to save the family property instead of moving anywhere easier, and to face down countless jokes at her expense, Eden squared her chin. She wanted Cade Sullivan, and by damn, she was going to have him.

"So what've you been up to lately?" he asked, leaning back in his chair. "Graduated high school, college. What else?"

"What else have I done since I graduated high school seven years ago?" she asked, snark overriding her seduction plans for a brief second. Thankfully her margarita arrived before she could say anymore. That gave Eden a second to mentally regroup. By the time Cade had said thanks for his beer, she'd decided on a plan.

It was one she figured Cade would approve of. Ready. Aim. Fire.

Ready.

She took a deep breath, the kind that added a little interest to the filmy fabric of her blouse, donned her sexiest, most seductive pout and leaned forward.

Aim.

"Do you know what I haven't done in, oh, I can't even remember how long?" she asked in a husky tone. The kind she'd use to share pillow talk, sex secrets and her favorite fantasy. The one that involved a naked Cade, the lake at midnight and a little light bondage.

Cade blinked. The neutral, aren't-you-a-cute-stranger

smile faded. He leaned back a little, like he wasn't sure what she might do next.

Fire.

"I haven't gone to the cliffs at night to watch the ocean," she told him. Unlike the lake, which had always been Cade's private love nest on his own property, the cliffs were just a mile away and open to the public. They were also a notorious makeout spot. She gave it a second for the words to sink in, for the visible tension to leave his shoulders, before reaching across the small table and running her fingernails gently over the back of his hand. "I love the power of the water at night, don't you? The crashing intensity. The uncontrolled, wild excitement. When was the last time you were on the cliffs, Cade? When was the last time you felt that kind of…excitement?"

Eden leaned back in her chair, lifting the margarita and sliding the bright pink straw between her teeth. Her eyes locked on his, she gently pursed her lips around the plastic and sucked.

"Mmm," she murmured before giving him a slow, inviting smile.

She put everything into that curve of her lips.

The heat of every fantasy.

The strength of every drop of sexual knowledge she had.

The hopes of every birthday wish she'd had since she was sixteen and first saw Cade Sullivan naked.

CADE WASN'T SURE what'd just happened.

One second, he was rolling nicely along, Eden playing her assigned part as the cute girl next door. The next, with just the flutter of those long eyelashes, she'd sent his body into overdrive.

This wasn't SOP.

And he was a guy who, once he'd decided on a course of action, followed standard operating procedures. His standards. His plan.

Neither of which included sporting a hard-on in the Wayfarers bar for a girl he'd already deemed off-limits. A girl who, whether she knew it or not, needed his help to keep from losing her home.

"Nope." He had to clear the desire from his throat before he continued. "No cliffside visits for me."

"That's too bad." Eden tilted her head to one side, a long silky strand of hair sliding over her cheek and down her throat like a caress before she tucked it away behind her ear. Her eyes, rich and dark, didn't leave his as she took another sip of her margarita.

Damn, she was good at that.

He licked his lips. Were hers as tasty as they looked?

Then something touched his leg. The slightest bump, then a slower, firmer press of her foot against his calf.

Cade damn near jumped out of his chair.

When had he lost control?

When had Eden become the kind of woman to take control?

And when had the entire idea become such a turn-on?

"So how's business?" he asked, shifting his legs a safe distance from hers. "You're working with animals, right? At the vet's or something?"

"I am the vet," she told him, slipping out of the seduction role for a second to give him a resigned look. "Maybe you missed it yesterday when you dropped me off? It's on my business card, too. The one I gave you with my phone number. You used it to call me to change times for this evening."

Cade winced. He wasn't sure which was better. To admit that he hadn't noticed anything except her the pre-

vious day. Or that he hadn't bothered to look at the card
because he'd had her phone number committed to memory for years.

"So, really? You're a vet?" That was a safe topic. And a
pertinent one, if he was going to figure out a way to help
her pay off his father. "That's hard to believe."

"Why is it so hard to believe? Don't you think I'm smart
enough? Good enough? Capable of keeping anything more
troublesome than a dandelion alive?" She rolled her eyes
before offering a disappointed shake of her head. "I didn't
think you were the kind to buy into rumors. Just because
I'm a little clumsy—and honestly, how it is that the few
accidents I do have these days only happen when you're
around is beyond me—does not mean I'm not great at
my job."

Ouch.

Sore subject?

He might not live here anymore, but Cade knew the
Ocean Point social games well enough to recognize a victim of them when he was lusting after her.

"That's not what I meant," he corrected with a frown.
It was probably better that she thought he saw her like everyone else. But he didn't like being lumped in with the
crowd, nor did he want her believing anything but the
truth. Even if the truth meant he'd have to work a little
harder to control his urge to grab her and kiss her like
crazy. "I just meant you're really young."

"I graduated veterinary school a year ago, then interned
in Sacramento for six months before opening my own
clinic," she said, her chin lifting a fraction as she gave
him a disappointed look.

"So you don't have to do four years of residency at a
local veterinary hospital in order to practice?" he teased.

"Maybe if I'd gone into veterinary surgery," she said,

relaxing enough to smile at him again. "My focus is on companion animals." At his questioning look, she added, "Pets."

"Cats and dogs."

"Mostly, yes. I've worked with small farm animals, too. Not that there's much call for that around here," she said with a shrug.

"Didn't I see a goat at your place yesterday?" he remembered.

"That's Jojo," Eden told him. Then, after a hesitant look, she pulled her cell phone from her purse. A couple of taps and she held it up to show off a picture of the goat and an elderly man. "She belonged to a guy named Lloyd Flanders. He passed on a few months back and nobody knew what to do with her, so she came to live with me."

"Was he a friend?"

"He was a curmudgeonly old grump who lived in a senior center and kept a goat for a pet," Eden said, laughing and suddenly looking even sexier than she had sucking on that straw. "I volunteer at the Gentle Hands society. It's a non-profit group that brings together pets and the elderly. Or, in this case, finds homes for pets when their elderly companions pass on. Pets are a wonderful way of keeping people involved in life. They bring a lot of joy and love and even a number of health benefits. But they grieve like people do when they lose someone."

He didn't know why, but hearing that was like a punch to the gut. Cade stared at his beer for a second, trying to reel in the images flashing through his mind. He knew what that was like. The pain of losing someone you cared about, the intense emptiness that ate away at you, leaving a hollow shell that felt like it could never be filled.

Suddenly, he was feeling mighty empathetic toward that goat.

"I'm sorry," Eden said suddenly, reaching across the table to brush a gentle caress over the back of his hand. "I didn't mean to bore you. I know not everyone is an animal fan."

"You didn't bore me," he denied. But she had given him an idea. If he could get his grandmother to adopt a pet, and to use Eden as her vet, he'd bet Catherine would persuade a few of her friends to do the same. It wasn't brilliant as far as finance schemes went, but given that Cade had spent most of his life trying to avoid educating himself in anything having to do with his father's profession, it wasn't a bad start.

First, though, he had to tell her about the loan.

Cade grimaced. He'd faced guerrilla insurgents with more enthusiasm than he could muster up right that second.

"So how's your mother doing these days?" he asked, figuring that was as good a segue as any. Right up until a rarely seen fury flashed in Eden's eyes. She looked like she might chew the flame off the tabletop candle.

Whoa. He quickly changed the subject back to animals, asking about the cat she'd found the previous day.

Ten minutes later, he'd have been hard-pressed to offer up proof of her claim that not everyone was an animal fan. While it'd all clearly been a guise to gather dirt for gossip, four people had stopped at their table under the guise of asking Eden various vet-related questions, from what her hours were to did she treat pigeons. A couple of groups had made their way over to welcome Cade home and used the *how is business, are you setting him up with a pet* gambit to try and see why the two of them were together.

When a large party, mostly made up of people he'd gone to high school with, came through the door, Cade gave up. There was no way he could talk to her about the loan here.

"Would you like to go?" he asked. "Maybe somewhere quieter where we can talk."

Eden sucked in her bottom lip for a second, then released it so the soft pillow of flesh glistened temptingly. Her lashes fluttered and soft color washed her cheeks before she nodded.

There she was. That sweet girl next door. Some of the tension that'd gripped Cade, mostly in the southern regions, eased.

Then she lifted her drink and wrapped those lips around the straw again, giving a long, gentle suck. Cade was pretty sure the instant rush of blood to his dick might be a health threat.

"I'd love to go somewhere else," she said agreeably, setting her empty glass on the table and giving him that look again. The one that said she was pretty sure she knew what he looked like nude, and was just as sure that once she got him that way, she intended to bring him to his knees.

Cade was so freaking tempted to let her. Except for two things.

One, she was Eden. And he had a strict policy against getting naked with good girls like her. The kind that came with strings and ties and expectations.

And two, she was *Eden*. Which meant he was probably imagining all the sexual innuendo. This heat, flaming toward an inferno, was probably all in his imagination. And his pants.

"I haven't been to the cliffs lately," she told him as she rose, the soft fabric of her blouse settling around her slender curves in a most intriguing way. "Why don't we head that way and see how they look tonight."

Cade blinked.

Uh-oh.

5

EDEN WANTED TO DO a giddy happy dance, but she was horribly afraid that, even sitting in the passenger seat of his car, she'd somehow fall right off these shoes and break her neck. So she settled on giving Cade a wide smile as he parked at the gates leading to the cliffs. When he shut off the car, she waited for him to do the gentlemanly thing, coming around to the passenger's side.

This was it. Her chance. She called on every seductive wile she had in her body, every naughty idea she'd garnered from years of reading sexy romance novels.

When he opened the door, she looked up to give him her most seductive look, then made sure her body brushed against his taller, harder one as she straightened. The contrast of feeling him against her softer curves was like an erotic charge shooting through her body with the intensity of an electrical current.

Her head spun just a little and heat pooled, damp and sticky, between her thighs. She'd never felt anything like this. The want. The need. Like the very air around them was fueling her passion.

"It's gorgeous tonight, isn't it," she said a little breathlessly, leaning against the car for a second to get her balance. And, if she were honest with herself, to clear her head. He was so intense, so gorgeous, and so mouth-wateringly sexy. But she could handle this. She might be a little—okay, a lot—out of her league, but she was a quick study.

"Gorgeous."

But he wasn't looking at the stars, or toward the cliffs, Eden noticed. He was staring at her.

Hoo-boy, she breathed. Maybe she couldn't handle this.

It wouldn't be the first time she'd overestimated her abilities.

But she'd never let overestimating, or worrying, slow her down. So she ignored the nerves and offered him a bright smile before taking her first step toward the cliffs.

Too bad she tripped.

"Careful," he said with a laugh, reaching out to take her hand and lead her oh-so-carefully toward the ocean's view.

Again with total gentlemanly concern.

She wondered if that translated to his sexual technique. Was he a gentleman there, too? Always letting the lady come first. What did it take to push him over the edge? To make him so crazy that he lost all control.

Could she find out? Did she have it in her?

For another brief second, she worried that she was in over her head. A cautious little voice in her mind warned that she could ruin things between them. That she'd forever lose her hero, the guy who always rode to her rescue. And there was the very real possibility that she'd end up disappointing at least one of them, if not both.

Of course, with her breaking some bones was always a possibility. Or, given her track record, she might send them both tumbling over the cliff into the ocean.

Then again, who better to take that dive with than a navy SEAL, she laughed to herself.

Lust and amusement shushed the little voice, shooing it back to the quiet corner where it belonged. She wanted Cade and this was her shot. She wasn't going to be scared away from it by silly little fears.

"Not too many people come this way anymore," she told him as they stepped carefully, the moonlight their only guide along the overgrown path. Her words weren't quiet, but they were still almost drowned out by the pounding crash of the ocean beyond. "The view is better up the coast, the hike a little easier. But I like it here."

"Me too," he said, giving her a cautious smile. Not like he was afraid of her, or worried, really. But like he knew she was up to something and just wasn't sure what trap she was about to spring. Eden didn't mind. His knowing that she was playing the game made it that much more interesting.

"So why do you like it here better?" he asked. "The lack of tourists? Because it's closer to home? Or does the less manicured, more wild nature appeal to you?"

"Sure. But really I like it here because it's makeout point," she told him with a wicked laugh, her fingers curling into his as he helped her over the log separating the parking area and the tall grasses leading west.

His fingers tensed around hers for a second, as if he was going to yank her against him. Then he released her hand and, with a charmingly distant smile, gestured that she take the lead.

Well, well. Wasn't he Mr. Military Control?

No problem. She had more weapons in her arsenal. She'd just have to play through them until she found the one that worked. That pushed him over the edge and broke that control.

As if testing her resolve, or her balance, Eden's shoe twisted on the dirt path, her ankle going in the opposite direction. She grimaced. Falling at his feet wasn't quite what she'd had in mind.

"Maybe we should head back," he suggested. "Come back in the daylight, to check out the cliffs. Maybe in tennis shoes."

"I'm good," Eden told him with a stubborn shake of her head. No way. It wasn't that she thought tonight was her only chance with Cade. But she wasn't positive how long she could make that worrisome, cautioning voice stay quiet. She'd learned a long time ago that if she wanted to have any fun, to do anything exciting, she had to stay one step ahead of that voice.

So she took the next curve more carefully, determined not to ruin her chance to be seen as something other than one of Cade's rescue projects.

Then her toes caught an exposed root. Her breath wooshed and her stomach spun as she stumbled. Cade's arm shot out, catching her before she lost her balance.

"Oops." She laughed, righting herself. "Maybe I should just try this barefoot."

"Here," he said with a rueful shake of his head. He reached out to pull her against him, his arm steadying her wobbling gait. "Hang on to me."

Her stomach was doing the tripping now, falling all over itself as her body shifted closer to his. She caught her breath, the salty brine air mixed with the scent of Cade's cologne. Ocean meets forest, all wrapped up in the heady possibilities of nighttime.

She leaned closer, shivering a little as her body aligned with his. Mmm, mmm, Eden hummed. Chalk one up for klutziness.

His legs were so long, reaching almost to her waist, even in her heels. The muscled strength of his arm was comforting, but steady around her shoulders. Her mind flooded with visions of his body, just as strong and steady, guiding her into all sorts of tricky sexual positions. Wasn't that going to be handy?

For a second, that little voice peeked out of the corner to warn Eden that she was crazy, and quite possibly morally questionable to be chasing after a guy simply for sex.

It wasn't just sex, she argued with herself. It was her only chance to live out the fantasy. To have this one last shot at Cade before she likely had to move and say goodbye for good.

The voice, probably stocking up its energy for *I told you so's,* scooted back into the quiet corner.

Leaving Eden to figure out how to go about her poorly planned seduction.

"Do you spend a lot of time at the ocean?" she asked, wondering what he did when he was living his real life. Besides all the hero stuff, of course. "I mean, navy, ocean. I know you probably see your fair share of water."

Cade's shrug was a lesson in delight, since it meant his chest did a subtle shift against the side of her breast. Eden's nipples perked up while desire stretched, like a waking cat, in her belly.

"Not so much anymore," he said. "I used to. A couple buddies and I spent a lot of time at the beach. Phil was from the Midwest, so being by the water was his idea of hanging out at a candy shop."

There was something in his words she'd never heard before. A heaviness. Her heart ached, though she didn't know why.

"Did he get tired of candy?" she teased as they reached the cliffs. The ocean, pounding power in the night, was a study of black noise. "Or did you just get tired of all the bikini-wearing babes throwing themselves at you?"

She felt his silent laugh against her shoulder.

"Does that ever get old?" he asked, sounding amused. But that…something. Pain? She wasn't sure what it was in his tone. But she wanted to fix it. To make it—and him—feel better.

Since he hadn't actually answered either of her questions, Eden waited. Even though they were still now, she didn't step out of his arms.

"Other than work, I don't go to the beach much these days," he finally admitted, his words so low they were almost carried away by the ocean breeze. Tension radiated from him, tight and edgy. Like he wanted to explode, but knew the damage would be catastrophic. Eden wondered what it was like, having that kind of control.

She didn't say anything. She just waited. But she did tighten her arm around his waist. It wasn't like she thought he *needed* her support. But she didn't mind offering it, just in case.

"We lost Phil last year," Cade finally said, his gaze locked on the churning waves. "I guess you'd call it a routine mission, although they never really are. He was taken out by shrapnel to the head. Never felt a thing."

No! Horrified, Eden's fingers tightened on his waist. She knew Phil was one of his best friends. Phil, a guy named Blake and Cade were in so many of the pictures Catherine loved to share. Once, about five years back, Cade had brought the two men home with him for the holidays. Eden hadn't met them, but had heard they were great guys. And in the few, rare times Cade ever spoke of his SEAL work, he always mentioned Blake and Phil.

To lose one of his best friends? He must be devastated.

"I'm so sorry," she whispered.

Beyond hurting for his loss, wondering how he was dealing with it, a fear she'd never felt took hold in Eden's gut. Cade was a hero. A SEAL. He went out and did the impossible, like Superman. To her, he'd always been invincible.

The sudden realization that he wasn't was terrifying.

"Hey, it's a risk of the job. We all face it," he said, shrugging and giving her that charming smile he'd perfected. A smile that pushed people away, she realized, her eyes widening in the dark. That smile put up a wall so solid, most people wouldn't even realize it was there.

He acted like it was no big deal. But she knew better. She couldn't imagine losing a best friend. A comrade in arms. One of Catherine's favorite photos was of a young Cade just out of boot camp. Eden was pretty sure one of the guys in that sterling framed picture was Phil. To lose that?

She took a deep breath. And here she'd been worrying about getting a little fantasy nookie before her life fell apart. What did that say about her?

"You're not gonna get all girly on me, are you?" he asked, looking down and giving her a laughing sort of shoulder nudge. Then he frowned and shifted, so he was standing in front of her instead of at her side.

She didn't realize she was crying until he reached out, sliding his index finger over her cheek to wipe away a tear.

"You're sweet," he said, his smile shifting. It was still charming. After all, was that gorgeous face capable of anything less? But there was a warmth there Eden hadn't seen before. Something beyond charm, that touched her heart. That scared the hell out of her.

"And you're a hero," she told him, trying for a teasing smile. It was a little shaky at the corners, but it was the best she could do.

"You ever think about setting aside those rose colored glasses?" he asked, a hint of cynicism shining through for a second before he pulled the charm back around him like a cozy blanket. "You're gonna get taken advantage of if you aren't careful."

She'd rather just be taken.

But for the first time since she'd hurled herself into this crazy plan to seduce Cade, she wondered if she really knew him.

Realizing she was on the verge of talking herself out of making a move, she figured it was now or never.

She wet her lips, then, before good sense could warn her to stop, she stood on tiptoe, her fingers pressed to his chest for balance, and brushed her lips over his.

Much like his goodbye peck the day before, it wasn't threatening. Instead it was soft. Gentle. Almost sweet, except for the needy aching heat it inspired low in her belly. For just a second, his lips moved against hers, welcoming. Warming.

She'd never wanted anything, *anyone,* like she did Cade Sullivan. Never needed anything more than for him to want her, too.

Eden slowly pulled back, her eyes searching his.

"Is that a belated thank-you for getting you out of the tree? Or a payment in advance for helping you walk back to the car without breaking a leg?" he teased, his expression more avuncular than hot and bothered.

She dropped back to her heels, working hard to keep from letting the pout take hold. That's it? She worked up all her nerve, finally made her first move and he brushed her off? Eden glared past Cade's shoulder, staring at the water while she tried to gather a little composure.

Give it up, she decided, wanting to cry again but for a very different reason this time. She forced herself to plaster a little fake cheer on her face and tried to smile as she looked up at him.

And saw something.

Maybe?

She peered closer.

He had that same chilly, distant smile going on. His expression was as neutral as Switzerland. But his eyes had a glow. Maybe it was the moonlight reflecting off the water, but she'd swear she saw heat there. Passion. Desire.

Her stomach tightened. Her breath caught and excitement swirled through her entire body.

He wanted her.

Oh, he clearly didn't want to want her.

But he did.

She should focus on the message in his smile, the coolness in his tone.

But it was so much more fun to see what she could do to encourage the passion in his gaze.

"Last week was my birthday," she said impulsively.

"Yeah?" Looking delighted at the safe subject, he gave her a playful shoulder pat. The kind you'd offer a puppy who'd finally mastered a clever trick. "Happy belated birthday, then. I hope you have a great year."

Eden knew he wanted her to stick with her friendly girl-next-door role. It was safer—he didn't have to worry about complicating things with sex. Or brushing her off, she reminded herself, trying to swallow past the imagined nasty taste rejection would leave. That was probably complicated, too. And not nearly as fun. She tilted her head to the side, grateful for the salty ocean breeze cooling her warm cheeks.

Safe route?

Or dive in with both feet.

"I think I will. You see, I made a birthday wish. It's the same wish I've made for the last handful of years."

"What's your wish?" he asked in a slow, cautious tone. Well, he wasn't a well-trained special ops guy for nothing.

"To have sex with you."

CADE WAS PRETTY SURE Eden could have kicked him in the balls at that moment and he wouldn't have felt a damned thing. Nope, his brain was frozen in shock, while his body was inflamed with need.

He gave a quick, contemplative glance at the cliffs. How far was the jump? He'd gone deeper—he'd probably survive. And it'd be less risky than what he faced at this moment.

Because right now, the threat wasn't the cute little brunette standing in front of him. Nope, it was his own desires. Desires he shouldn't feel, knew better than to entertain and usually pretended didn't exist.

Cade had rules. Strict ones that he lived his relationships by. The first being that there were no strings involved. Past, present or future. And with Eden, Cade had lifelong relationship ties that went all the way back to hauling her off her trike when she'd run it into the bushes at the base of his driveway.

They had a history.

They had a friendship. The closest he'd ever had with a woman.

What they shouldn't have was heat. Passion. Sexual needs that arced between them like a live electric current, threatening to burn down anything it touched.

"Look…"

What?

How did he explain his rules? Ask her to promise not to get ugly when he walked away? To accept that once he walked, they wouldn't be playing again the next time he was home? To other women, it was easy. But to Eden? He'd sound like a prick. And while he might laugh off her always calling him her hero, he wasn't excited about the idea of destroying that myth *and* hurting her feelings all at the same time.

"Poor Cade," she laughed, like she thought it was funny that she'd tied him in knots then forced him to choose between his morals and his body's pounding needs. "It's hard, isn't it?"

Oh, baby, she had no idea.

Then her gaze changed. Went from amused to smoldering. She leaned back a little and made a show of giving him a long look. Down. Then up. Then back down again.

His dick throbbed. Her actions were probably some kind of sexual Morse Code for *do me and do me now.*

"Hmm," she murmured, those luscious full lips smiling now. Not the friendly smile he was used to, either. This one was pure sexual challenge. It was like she could read his mind. Which only added to the needy ache pressing against his zipper.

"All you have to do is tell me you don't want me," she said, giving him a look of sweet challenge through her lashes. As if testing his resolve, and daring him to lie straight to her face, she stepped closer.

Close enough that the tips of her breasts brushed his chest. That her breath was warm on his face. That he could see the sparkling humor in her dark eyes.

That was the thing that slayed him about Eden. No matter what was going on, what current disaster she'd dropped herself into, she always found a way to laugh. To enjoy herself.

Why the hell was that so sexy?

Why was she so damned irresistible?

"Look," he tried again. What had she said he could do to make her back off? He couldn't remember.

"Haven't you ever been a birthday wish before?" she asked when he couldn't find any words—or thoughts—to stop her. "Something you really, really wanted and knew you couldn't get yourself. Something that was going to take a little bit of magic."

"There's no such thing as magic," he managed to grind out as he tried to keep from moving too much. Every breath was a lesson in torture, pressing his chest closer against those soft, gloriously full breasts. He wanted to touch them. To feel them. To weigh them in his palms while running his thumbs over her nipples.

Oh, God. Her nipples. Nothing turned Cade on more than a set of gorgeous breasts.

"You don't believe in magic?" Upping the torture, she traced the fingertips of one hand up his arm, a whisper-soft journey toward his shoulder. Then she changed the angle, so her nails scraped ever-so-gently down his chest. "I think it's very real. Some might call it luck. That special something that brings everything and everyone into the right place at the right time so something special can happen."

"We make things happen," he said, barely aware of his words since the few drops of blood that weren't pounding their way south were totally focused on her fingers, now winding a path of torture around his hardening nipple.

"Of course we do," she agreed, her eyes molten now. So hot, so filled with passion and power that he was surprised they weren't shooting flames. Talk about magic. All she had to do was give him that look and he was done. All of the rules, all good sense, gone.

"But since I did build up a lot of years of birthday candle wishes, don't you think it's about time we made some *very* good…"

Pressing closer, close enough that he could feel her nipples through her bra, she stood on tiptoe.

"Things."

She scattered whisper-soft kisses along his jaw, her warm breath a vivid contrast to the cool ocean breeze.

"Happen."

Her teeth scraped along his throat. Cade growled. Sweet he could resist. But this sexy side of naughty?

He had no more willpower.

It was like she'd found the key to the part of him he kept locked tight. The part he mostly denied. The part that wanted her, wanted a future, believed he could actually have a relationship. The part that pretended the statistics regarding military relationships didn't apply to him. That he could beat the odds. That he wanted to try.

Or, more likely, she'd hit his horny button and he was about to explode.

Either way, there was no holding back any longer.

6

GRABBING EDEN BY THE WAIST, Cade pulled her tight against his hips, grinding his hard, throbbing dick against her soft warmth. He took her mouth. His lips slanted, finding the right angle, pressing and sliding against hers. Why did she fit so perfectly? Her mouth opened to his, inviting him in with a soft moan.

His tongue swept in, testing.

Tasting.

She was delicious.

His hands rushed over her body with desperate haste. She, on the other hand, was taking the slow, leisurely route, her palms smoothing his biceps before her nails scraped the muscle gently. He shivered. Freaking shivered. He'd been with plenty of women. A lot who saw his body as a damned fine example of masculine perfection.

But he'd never felt worshipped before.

Never felt that this—the sex—was as much about him as it was the end result. Doing it with a SEAL. Doing it with a Sullivan. Getting to the orgasm.

But Eden was all about him.

The real him.

Cade wasn't sure what swelled more at that thought. His ego or his dick.

Said dick did a little throbbing dance in his pants, as if to yell, *Yo, dude. This is my time. Egos check it at the zipper.*

Taking his cue from below, Cade focused.

On Eden.

She was perfect. Her mouth fit his like they'd been made for each other, her lips gliding over his mouth in a whisper-soft caress that seduced all the more because of its sweetness.

On her body.

It was delicious. Soft, curvaceous and welcoming as she snuggled up against him.

On how she made him feel.

Like the hero she joked he was. Like he could do anything, be anything, because she believed in him. Like making her feel as incredible as he did. Like giving her the kind of sensual delights that would blow her mind, make her scream with pleasure, send her body melting into orgasmic overload.

Yeah. He could do all that.

He took the kiss deeper.

Slower.

Their tongues danced, sliding hot and slick against each other. In and out, twirling and licking. The dance was slow. Sensually sweet. Cade felt like he was spinning in a gentle eddy, floating softly around the edges of passion as it pulled them in tighter, closer to the center.

He relaxed as the cool ocean breeze skimmed his bare arms, wondering when he'd ever felt this mellow during a kiss. Usually it was all hard, driving force, with passion pounding, demanding, taking control.

This was nice.

Sweet.

Easy.

Then Eden shifted, her fingers digging into his shoulders and her breasts pressing, hard, against his chest. Cade's body reacted like she'd just poked at his passion meter with a cattle prod. She sucked his tongue deep inside her mouth. He growled, every single muscle in his body going rock hard. It was like an inward orgasm. Sensation exploded inside Cade, making him quake with desire. His fingers shook as his hands raced down her back, cupping her ass and pulling her tight against his throbbing erection. Her moan reverberated against his tongue, adding a whole new dimension of pleasure to the delights she was offering.

She wrapped one leg around his thigh, so her hot core was pressed against him. He was breathing like a freight train now, desperate, needy, craving her like a drug he couldn't live without.

Holy hell. He'd thought she was nice and sweet?

Clearly, Eden knew a thing or two about torture.

On the edge of losing all semblance of control—and with it the image he always carefully maintained in Ocean Point that he was a gentleman—Cade pulled back. Just a little. Enough to see the passion fogging her dark eyes, to delight in the sexual need clear on her face.

Her need for him.

A need he was suddenly desperate to satisfy.

"You know what I like?" she asked quietly, her head falling backward, leaving the long line of her throat bare in the moonlight. "I like having my nipples tweaked. I want to feel what it's like to have you suck them into your mouth. To swirl your tongue around and nibble on them."

Cade was pretty sure his brain exploded right then and there. His knees almost gave out. His dick pounded against his zipper, determined to get out and play.

All this time, he'd figured her for a sweet, shy girl next door. Instead she was a sexual siren, a seductress with amazing sensual powers. It was like she'd delved into his deepest sexual fantasies and decided to bring them to life.

"I'll bet you taste delicious," he muttered, stepping back so he could clearly see her body, hidden in moonlight and fabric. He couldn't do much about the lack of lighting, but he could damned sure get rid of the material.

His fingers made frantic work of the buttons of her blouse, spreading the filmy fabric wide. Her skin glowed like white silk in the moonlight, a vivid contrast against her red bra. Cade traced the curve, just there, where the satin was edged in black ribbon. His mouth watered. He wanted to taste her. All of her.

But he knew his limits.

Her breath was coming faster now, those satin covered breasts quivering with every inhalation. Cade wanted to rip the red bra away. To touch, to taste. But he couldn't. The minute the bra came off, he'd lose every last bit of control.

So he feasted on her breasts with his eyes, but kept his mouth away. And his hands occupied.

Otherwise he'd take her with hard, fast desperation.

For no other woman would he ignore most of his rules of engagement so he could feast on her sexiness. But this was Eden. His sweet girl next door. The one who'd haunted his dreams for years. He had to taste her. Just a little taste. He had to hear her come, just once. But that was it. Just once, just a taste. He couldn't have more—wouldn't allow himself satisfaction—until he'd talked to her about expectations, made sure she knew the rules.

And there was no way in hell he was having that talk right now, with her body so hot and ready for him.

Unable to resist any longer, he cast a quick, desperate look around. There, ten feet to the north, was a crop of rocks. Picnickers used them, he remembered. They'd be good enough, except he had a different treat in mind.

"Over here."

He didn't wait for her to follow.

He simply swept her into his arms and carried her across the rocky ground.

"Afraid I'll fall at your feet?" she teased, her hands sweeping around the back of his neck, fingers tickling the hair at his nape.

Cade grinned down at her, suddenly feeling more like the romantic hero she saw him as than the horny guy in a hurry he knew he was.

"More afraid I'll fall at yours," he admitted, sinking his face into the silky strands of her hair and breathing deep before setting her gently on the broad stone surface. "You're a handful."

"Surely I'm not too much for you?" she asked, her tone not teasing anymore. Cade had to wonder what kind of guys she'd been hanging out with to ask such a crazy question.

Instead of answering, or releasing her, he held her gaze with his, refusing to let her look away. He leaned in slowly, taking her mouth with his. Softly at first. Just a glide of lips over lips.

She sighed.

He slipped his tongue along the edge of her teeth, sucking gently on the full pillow of her lower lip.

She whimpered.

He plunged his tongue deep, in and out, intense and fast.

Her nails bit into the back of his neck as she hung on, groaning in delight.

Cade shifted, angling his body to bump his hips against her knees. As if she'd been reading his mind forever, she shifted, clamping one thigh on either side of his and pulling him closer.

He'd found heaven, right here between her legs.

Suddenly desperate to explore more, Cade let go of Eden's waist, his hands rushing over her hips and down the fabric of her skirt to find the soft flesh of her thighs.

"Your hands are so warm," she breathed against his mouth. "So strong."

"Shh," he told her, releasing her mouth to trail tiny kisses down her throat. His hand skimmed up her thigh, under that tight little skirt. "You talk, you forfeit the fun."

"You mean you're calling all the shots?" she clarified, the last word coming out a squeak when his finger found the edge of her panties.

"I plunder, you surrender," he confirmed with a grin. She caught on fast.

"I never surrender," she breathed as his fingers curled under the elastic, sweeping inward, combing through her damp curls.

"Sure you will," he vowed.

He was going to make sure of it.

EDEN HAD SPENT a lot of time over the years imagining her and Cade together. She'd written stories in her mind, created visual odes to sexual pleasure starring the two of them.

She'd had no clue.

Not a freaking single one.

He was amazing. Incredible. He was going to ruin her for every other man for the rest of her life. And she didn't care. After all, just the fantasy of him had ruined her for all men up until this point. Why ruin a perfect track record?

His hands were so hot, his fingers sure as they skimmed

her thigh, teasing their way under the edge of her panties. Her body throbbed, wet, needy.

She wiggled a little, trying to entice his fingers. Hoping he'd touch her. Needing him to relieve the pressure that was building, tight as a spring, low in her belly.

He angled himself between her thighs, lifting her with both hands and scooting her further up the rock. The contrast of his warm body, hard muscles and unforgiving stone added an extra erotic edge to the passion coursing through her. His hand swept down her legs to her ankles, making her shiver as he gripped her feet just above the little leather straps of her shoes. Still gripping her ankles, he lifted her feet so they rested flat on the rock with her knees aimed at the sky.

"I feel like a sacrifice to the sea gods," Eden laughed breathlessly, propping herself up on her elbows to watch him through passion-hazed eyes. He looked so hot, so sexy. And so much better pleasuring her up close than he'd ever looked with someone else far away.

"They'd have parted the water for you," he told her before pressing an open mouth kiss against her knee, just inside where it curved. She shivered, delight skimming up her thigh like hot water over a hot skillet. With his eyes locked on hers, he kept the kisses climbing. She held her breath, her body getting tenser the higher he climbed. By the time he reached the tautly stretched fabric of her skirt, she was ready to pass out from lack of oxygen.

As he continued pressing kisses up her thigh, he slid the material higher with his palms, skimming their hard warmth along the outside of her legs as he went. He felt so good, those fingers so powerful and strong against her soft flesh.

"You're gorgeous," he said, his words husky and low, hanging on the night air.

"You're looking at me in the dark," she teased.

"I've got excellent night vision. And even better night skills." He pushed her skirt up to her waist, so her cherry-red thong was on full view. Even with the moon behind him, she could still see the glint of passion in his gorgeous eyes.

"Night skills?" she asked, her words hitching higher when her now-bare butt settled back down on the cold stone. "Is that a military thing?"

"Why don't we find out," he told her, lifting her legs and draping both knees over his shoulders. "You ready to surrender?"

Surrender? Eden wasn't sure she could even think.

Had she ever been in such an erotic position? Had a man ever looked at her like he was going to eat her alive, and make sure she loved every second of it?

She'd haul out the white flag and wave it like crazy.

Except then the game would be over.

"Oh, no," she breathed instead. She gave him her best *go ahead, I dare you* look. "You haven't won yet."

"Maybe not. But you're about to," he promised.

Then he got down to the feast.

His hands cupped the firm flesh of her butt, lifting her to the perfect angle for his mouth.

Keeping it slow, reining in the desperation, he used his tongue. Licked a wet path from the inside of her knee, all the way to her now sopping wet curls. Breathing in, as if he were addicted to her musky scent, he blew a puff of air against the quivering flesh between her thighs.

Eden gasped. Her fingers curled, then uncurled, like she was trying to grab the rock.

He slid his tongue along her clitoris.

Eden moaned.

He slipped one finger, then two, into her hot, aching depths. Swirling, pressing, then sliding back out.

Oh, baby.

He was incredible.

She wanted him like crazy. More, she wanted him to want her. To ache for her. To be more desperate for her than he'd ever been for anyone else in his life. Eden wanted to be special.

That need, that hope, overcame all of her inhibitions.

Remembering the intensity in his eyes when he'd looked at her breasts, the way he'd reached for them then stopped himself, she reached behind her back and unhooked her bra.

Quick, with a grace she rarely showed in anything else, she slipped out of her blouse and bra, then lay back on the stone again so her body was bared to the night sky, the ocean air, and Cade's hot eyes.

"Holy hell," he breathed against her thigh. She wasn't sure if the new wetness there was her own dripping juices, or if he was drooling.

Oh, please, her fragile ego begged. Let him drool over her.

With that in mind, she cupped her own breasts, using every move she wanted him to do on herself. She squeezed. She ran the tip of her fingers around her sensitive areola. She scraped her nail across the pebbled nipple, making herself gasp.

She could feel his eyes on her breasts. They were hot, intense as he watched from below. Even more turned on by his stare than she was with her own ministrations, she worked herself harder, her fingers swirling, plucking, teasing. His tongue swirled, plunged, sipped in time with her movements. She set the pace. She held all the control. She'd never had this much power, this much pleasure.

Then she cupped both breasts in her palms, the nipples jutting between her knuckles as she squeezed. Her hands worked the soft mounds, heating her own flesh as the cool ocean breeze nipped at the beaded tips in an erotic contrast. Her moans rose, her butt along with them as she pressed closer to his mouth, entreating him to take her higher.

His tongue stabbed, in and out. His thumb worked her throbbing clitoris, pressing, then skimming the swollen surface.

Her breath came in pants now. Her body rose higher. Her mind shut down. All she could do was feel.

His teeth nipped.

She exploded.

A fireworks of stars bombarded her closed lids, her head full back against the hard rock as she dug her heels into Cade's shoulders to press herself higher. To wring every drop of ecstasy out of the orgasm.

She just kept coming and coming.

Wave after wave of sensations poured through her body.

In time with the crashing ocean below, the power of her climax was overwhelming. It was like being swept away on a sea of passion, helpless against the intensity.

Slowly, so so slowly, she floated back into her body. Awareness seeped in as she felt Cade's body, still between her thighs. His hands slowly caressed her thighs, her butt. Like he was gently guiding her back.

Her own fingers soothed now, petting her exhausted flesh, warming her nipples as the passion eased, as her body settled.

"Wow," she finally breathed. "As in, oh, my God. Wow."

Cade's laugh sounded pained. Like he was hurting.

Poor baby.

Eden forced her eyes open, using every bit of strength she had to tilt her head upright. Her lashes fluttered, eyelids so heavy as she forced them open to stare at her sexy hero.

The skin was taut across his face, as if he was facing high levels of pain. If his body was anywhere near as turned on as hers had been, he probably was.

And she was just the girl to take care of that for him.

Excitement giving her new levels of energy, Eden's mind raced with all the things she wanted to do to him. On that body. Oh, baby.

She sat up, shoving her bra and blouse aside. She didn't care that her skirt was bunched up around her waist and her panties probably feeding the sharks in the ocean below.

"Yum," she said with a soft laugh. "I have to admit, I think you got my surrender there. But now it's your turn."

CADE'S ERECTION PRESSED against the stone's surface, throbbing so hard he was surprised it didn't jackhammer the surface to dust.

Before it took over, snapping his tenuous hold on control, he pushed away from the rock and put some much needed distance between him and Eden.

"What...?" Her shock was clear as the words rang out in question.

He was in trouble.

He'd gone over the side of an aircraft carrier once. He'd had total faith in himself, his training and his calculations. Still, there had been one brief second when he'd jumped that he'd questioned his own sanity. The dive had taken forever, and had been over in an instant.

That's how he felt now.

Like he was in over his head, and no matter how much he thought he was controlling the situation, there was every chance that it could all go to hell as soon as he landed.

She was five feet away, and yet, it was like she was still wrapped around him.

He could taste her, rich and heady, on his tongue.

He could feel her, soft and welcoming, against his body.

Her cries of delight, low and husky, would echo through his dreams tonight.

She was...

Wow.

And she was sliding off the rock and coming his way.

Oh, God.

Her skin glowed white in the moonlight, a vivid contrast against the black skirt she'd thankfully tugged into place. Her berry-red nipples were still swollen, well-worked by her skilled fingers.

Cade tried to shove his hands in the front pockets of his slacks, but the fabric was pulled so taut, they wouldn't fit. So he settled on crossing his arms over his chest and glaring at the ocean.

"Is that how it's supposed to end?" Eden asked, her tone a combination of amusement and sexy contentment as she came closer. She didn't touch him, thankfully. He wasn't sure his slacks could handle it. But she stopped close enough that her scent, honeysuckles again, invaded his senses. Close enough that he could feel the warmth radiating off her slender body.

End? It shouldn't have started. God, what was he thinking? He was supposed to be telling her about the loan his father was calling in. He should be helping her fix the mess her mother had left, one she didn't even know was about to crash down on her.

Instead, he'd gone down on her in a public park.

Wasn't he a prince.

"That's how it should end," he said. Then he realized how callous that sounded and almost groaned aloud. This was why he never did good girls—especially not here, in his hometown. He always stuck with ones who knew the game plan well before the panties were torn off.

But it was too late. Eden's panties were who knew where, and she was looking at him like she wasn't sure if he was the greatest thing since milk chocolate or a big mean ogre who was about to ruin her dreams.

He knew he should take the ogre route. He should be a hard-ass, tell her the way things were, and apologize for not filling her in before he'd stuck his tongue inside her body.

He should let his mistake be the perfect excuse to end things quickly and cleanly, before they got complicated. Or ugly.

Except this was Eden.

So things were already complicated. And he never, ever wanted to make her life ugly.

So instead of explaining, even nicely, why this had been a mistake, he did the most stupid thing ever.

He pulled her into his arms. Still staring at the ocean beyond, he sighed.

"I've got to get back to the hospital," he lied. "So I guess only one of us gets to win tonight."

Unable to resist, he brushed a kiss over her soft hair and added, "Sorry, babe. It was incredible."

7

THE NEXT DAY Eden sat at her desk, staring out at the green fields beyond the barn that served as her veterinary clinic and swore she could still feel tiny little aftershock orgasms. And she had to assume, given that it'd essentially been a solo party, that on the sexual Richter scale that'd been an average quake. She couldn't wait to find out what a full-blown, totally naked, penetration-rocks explosion was going to feel like.

"The question is," she murmured to the dog weaving between her feet and the chair legs, "will I get to find out? Cade wasn't exactly beating the drum for a do-over last night."

It was more like he was doing his damnedest to hurry her along before she got ideas. Either sticky ones that would require him to make excuses, or dramatic girly ones that would inspire him to run like hell.

But she hadn't done either. After he'd practically carried her back to the car, since she was even less sturdy on her high heels after he'd rocked her world, they'd kept up small talk. Friendly, meaningless social chitchat, as they'd both been raised to excel in. Then he'd walked her to the door, brushed a kiss over her lips and hurried off to see his father in ICU.

She'd wanted to ask if that was just an excuse, since everyone knew Cade wasn't a big fan of his father. And she wasn't sure if ICU was open at ten at night. But for a Sullivan, usual rules never applied. The insecure part of her, the one she tried to pretend didn't exist, had immediately wondered if Cade regretted their little love-fest.

The rest of her, the part that liked to dive headfirst into life and deal with the fallout later, shrugged off the worry. What good would it do to obsess? If he'd hated it, she'd deal with that when she saw him.

Or she'd sit here and freak out.

Sighing, Eden chewed on her thumbnail, wishing the knotted nerves in her stomach would unravel enough so she could eat something more nutritious for lunch.

A late lunch at that, since her clinic had had people in and out all day. Other than the three scheduled appointments, she'd had seven visitors, all casually moseying through to see how her day was coming along.

The first three had amused her. They'd all been schoolmates from town who'd wanted to congratulate her on trading up. Trading from what, she wasn't sure. The next two visitors were harmless irritations, both social-climbing hangers-on who were clearly looking for something juicy to make them popular with the Oceanfront ladies. But the last two, who Eden actually didn't know, had apparently learned their interviewing skills from the paparazzi. Or the inquisition.

Since none of them had pets, or the brains to pretend they might be checking into her services as well as her personal life, she didn't feel bad about sending them away without a speck of fuel for their gossip.

Now she was hiding with the stack of files sent to her

by local animal shelters and groups. The Shady Acres Retirement Home had five new residents this month and Eden wanted to visit in the morning with a list of possible pets for them to adopt.

"Eden…?"

Trying not to growl, Eden laid down her pen and eyed the dog.

"Think we can pretend we're not here?" she asked the small gray mutt. "Because you know, they're only after gossip."

"Eden?" the voice called, louder and more insistent.

"Back here," she admitted, rising resignedly to meet the eighth interruption of the morning. "In the office."

Some—mostly the Oceanfront set—would say that calling a small room in a barn an office was a little on the ambitious side. But, hey, it had a desk, a phone and internet access. A few framed certificates, her veterinary license and a huge orange filing cabinet completed the office requirement checklist.

"Oh, there you are, dear," the older woman said breathlessly, reaching the doorway before Eden had even crossed the small room. Eden eyed the stubby legs beneath that vivid floral dress. Had she run?

"Hi, Mrs. Carmichael," she greeted cautiously.

"I brought Paisley in," the heavyset woman said, stating the obvious since the cat was draped over her shoulders. She, not the cat, glowered at Mooch, who was cowering behind Eden's feet. "I don't want her scared, though."

"She got to know Mooch the other day when she was here visiting," Eden said cheerfully, holding out her fingers for the cat to sniff. With a jaw-snapping yawn, the feline arched her back, then stood on her owner's shoulder to leap into Eden's arms.

"Whoa, well, hello," Eden said with a laugh, falling

back a step under the sudden weight of the cat. "Aren't you the sweetheart? And a take-charge sweetheart, at that."

Impressed that the older woman could cart the twenty-pound feline around like she did, Eden decided comfort was more important than trying to prove she was as strong as a sixty-year-old. Hooking her foot around the wheel of her chair, she pulled it over next to the visitors' chair. Just in case Mrs. Carmichael was the stay-close-to-her-pet type.

As soon as they settled—Eden with the cat in her lap—Mooch came over and stood, front paws on Eden's legs, to say hi.

"Watch that," Mrs. Carmichael cautioned, half rising as if to throw herself between the dog and cat.

Eden's heart, always a sucker for anyone who loved animals, went soft.

"She'll be okay," she promised. But she put a cautioning hand on the dog's collar, just in case.

It only took two sniffs before the cat was purring and rubbing her white-spotted face against the dog's ear.

"Well, will you look at that?" Mrs. Carmichael gave the pair a baffled glance before turning, wide-eyed to Eden. "She never gets along with other animals. Or people, for that matter."

"Savannahs are known for being cautious," Eden agreed, rubbing her knuckle under the feline's chin. The cat was not only purring like a motorboat now, but doing the comfy circle dance in Eden's lap. "But once they make a bond, it's a pretty tight one."

"Hmm."

"What's wrong?" Eden asked, smiling at the grumpy-faced older woman.

"I didn't realize you were quite so well-read on rare cats. Or that you had such a way with animals."

"It is my job," Eden added, figuring it was easier to

smile than to grind her teeth. Even though that would have felt a hell of a lot better. What was up with people? They thought they had her so easily pegged? *Nice-enough misfit, a little klutzy, always good for a laugh.*

"Well, yes, but I suppose I thought you mostly tended animals like this one." The older woman gestured to Mooch, who was sniffing around her shoes like they were made of bacon.

"I try not to discriminate," Eden said gently, offering the raggedy looking mutt an indulgent look, even as she continued to rub her fingers under the chin of a cat that cost more than her car. "Mooch was abandoned when his owner died. He'd been with her for twelve years, and in the end, he was her only companion. Her only company. When she had a stroke, he shredded a window screen to escape, ran back and forth in front of the house, barking until he got someone's attention."

Mrs. Carmichael's polished lips rounded as she looked—actually *looked*—at the dog.

"All the owner's family wanted when she was gone was her money, anything they could sell for profit. They were going to have the dog put down."

"No!"

As if Eden had just taken a gun and aimed it at the canine, the older woman snatched him up and cuddled his wriggling body close in her arms.

"It happens a lot," Eden said sadly. She hated that. Hated that she couldn't do more to stop it. Her estimation of the other woman had sure taken a high leap, though. "The shelters, rescue groups and other vets know I take in special cases and try to find them homes. One of them called me about Mooch and I convinced the new owners to let me keep him."

"Does he have a home, then?"

Hmm. Quickly shielding her considering look, Eden shook her head slowly, letting her chin droop just a little. "He doesn't. I'm trying to find him one, though. I can't keep too many dogs here myself—it's just not fair to them."

Mooch, the consummate player, chose that moment to lick the older woman's chin and give a friendly yip. Mrs. Carmichael laughed, hugging him close.

"Well, that's a shame. I can't bring a dog home myself because Mr. Carmichael is allergic. But I have friends…"

Eden grinned.

Mooch was as good as placed. Mrs. Carmichael had a reputation for never saying anything she didn't mean—and quite a bit she did but should keep to herself. And given the tax bracket of her friends, Eden figured Mooch stood a really good chance of finishing out his golden years in prime style.

Five minutes later, Mooch on her lap, Mrs. Carmichael finally wound her way around to the real purpose of her visit.

"I heard that sweet boy, Cade Sullivan, helped you rescue my Paisley."

Sweet boy? Eden's lips twitched.

"Actually I'd already rescued Paisley. Bev was in the car giving her water when Cade showed up," she corrected meticulously. Then she laughed and leaned forward to admit, "It was me Cade was rescuing."

Mrs. Carmichael's eyes rounded, right along with her mouth.

"I figure you're here to get the really good inside dirt, right? And only Bev, Cade and I know that part. So there you go, I've just provided you with lunch fodder for an entire week." Too amused to be offended, Eden grinned.

The older woman tried for a look of righteous indignation, but couldn't hold it for more than a few seconds. Smiling back, she reached over to pat Eden's hand. "Sweetie, you're the best gossip this year. You didn't think I was going to waste my advantage, did you? Especially not when I've got the inside track."

"Is Paisley your inside track, then? I should charge you for an office visit for this," Eden teased, her fingers combing through the cat's soft fur. The Savannah purred her approval. Surprisingly, so did Mrs. Carmichael in the form of a harrumphing hum.

"Good point." The older woman looked around the office, noting the various animal photos, inspecting the certificates and then giving Eden a considering look. "Why don't you go ahead and give my baby a checkup. Make sure she's faring well after her little adventure. We'll see how that goes."

For a solid heartbeat, Eden just stared. What? A real appointment? From one of the Oceanfront matrons? Warning herself not to get too excited, Eden scooped the cat up into her arms and tilted her head to one side to ask, "Adding legitimacy to your pending story?"

The older woman laughed, rising too and waiting for Eden to lead the way to an exam room. "I'm meeting the Spring Fling planning committee in the morning. And you have to admit, your rescue and subsequent examination of my baby gives me an exciting co-star status in gossip central's latest favorite topic."

"Well…" Eden set the still purring cat on a stainless table and, one hand still rubbing her ears, reached for the stethoscope, "I think Paisley's the actual co-star."

"I'm her agent," Mrs. Carmichael deadpanned.

"She's a lucky cat," Eden decided ten minutes later after giving the cat a thorough and surprisingly easy exam. Savannahs weren't known for being agreeable, but the feline, who weighed more than Mooch, had purred through the entire checkup. "And in excellent health. You might want to supplement her with some fish oil. Omega-3s are good for the immune system and will make her coat even shinier. From the scent of her fur, you're taking her to the salon Dr. Turner recommends. They're lovely and do a fabulous job of pampering the pets. But after a month on the fish oil, you won't need those conditioning baths. Also, Savannahs often have a taurine deficiency, so if you aren't already, you might want to begin supplementing."

"I suppose you sell this taurine?"

Eden looked up from her inspection of the feline's nails to shake her head. "No, but I can recommend a few brands, though."

Mrs. Carmichael gave another humming humph, then nodded.

"You're very good at that," she decided with a considering look. "Paisley doesn't take to most people, let alone veterinarians. She hates the techs at Dr. Turner's. They've started asking me to sedate her before visits."

"Oh, that's a shame," Eden said, giving the huge cat a sympathetic hug. "I know Savannahs can be considered persnickety, but you'd think a veterinary clinic would understand that about the breed."

"You'd think," the other woman murmured before asking about the charges.

Eden gave the cat one last scratch, then leaving her with her owner, stepped over to the computer to print out a bill.

"So, where did you and the sweet Sullivan boy go after drinks last night?" Mrs. Carmichael asked, making a show of pulling her checkbook out of her Hermès bag. "A walk on the cliffs, perhaps?"

"Oh, my God," Eden breathed, the bill hanging limp in her fingers. Horrified images of YouTube videos, Instagrams and mocking humiliation for not moaning correctly during an orgasm all filled her head. "Did someone follow us?"

The older woman laughed so hard she snorted. Then, after wiping a tear from one eye, she took the paper and patted Eden's hand.

"Sweetie, you are such a rookie at this."

Eyes huge, Eden shook her head in denial. "That was a setup? But how'd you guess?"

"Process of elimination. Cade's BMW headed west when he left the Wayfarers. That meant you either went to the cliffs or up the coast. Since word is that his car was in his driveway two hours later, the cliffs were the best bet."

"We could have circled around, made a turn somewhere."

"Cade's too practical for that, sweetie. Please, if you don't know him better than that, how are you going to keep people guessing about what happened?"

Before Eden could process that, or even wonder if she'd totally underestimated the depth and reach of the Ocean Point gossip chain, the other woman handed her a check.

Eden glanced at the amount, then forcibly yanked her jaw off the floor.

"Um, I think this is a mistake." She tried to hand the slip of paper, with its overabundance of zeros, back.

"That's for the rescue, and the reward I'd have had to offer. For today's visit, which I'm assuming since it's a Sunday and your posted hours don't include weekends, means this is considered emergency time, and a retainer for monthly checkups for the next three months. At that point, we'll reevaluate."

With a grunt, she lifted the twenty pound feline, draped her over her shoulder like a purring stole, and gave Eden a nod.

"I'll be in touch during regular business hours to set up

Paisley's schedule. I'll expect you to have those supplements you recommended for me then, too. And don't forget to have Mooch ready for visitors. I'll send a few people out to meet him."

Between the buzzing in her ears and the feeling of standing on a very unstable cloud, Eden was sure she said something. Hopefully it included the words "thank you" and maybe "goodbye." But she couldn't be sure.

Still standing there in shock, Eden stared after the departing floral steamship.

Then she looked at the check again.

She'd done it.

Oh, she hadn't saved her home yet. But she'd gotten a new client. One who was married to the bank owner's brother, and had just handed her enough to pay off one-thirtieth of the loan.

Hips swinging, Eden happy-danced her way back to her office.

She'd told Bev that dating Cade should bring in some gossip gawkers who'd use their pets as an excuse to troll for dirt. But she'd just said that to throw Bev off Eden's true dating intentions. She hadn't really believed it.

But now?

"Mooch, we just might make this work after all," she said, tossing the dog a treat. Then, figuring if anything deserved celebrating, this did, she dug into her emergency chocolate stash and had one herself.

A screaming orgasm, a possible home for Mooch and a wealthy new client. This weekend was working out pretty darned good.

8

CADE WASN'T SURE what it'd take to make the weekend much worse. A plague, maybe. A natural disaster or two.

Or another visit to the hospital.

"Your father is out of ICU now. He's all settled in a private room and getting a little testy with the doctors' order that he not have a computer or work-related paperwork. After this morning's incident, they even restricted his access to the newspaper," Catherine said with a worried frown. Moving with the ease of someone much younger than her eighty years, she bustled around the brightly lit kitchen. Pouring coffee into a large custom mug with a picture of a fluffy baby harp seal and the caption *My Grandson*, she handed it, and a plate of cookies, to Cade. Then she gestured that he take them to the sitting room.

"I'm sure he's fine," Cade said absently, waiting until she took her cup of tea—in fine china with no seal—and was settled into her favorite chair before taking his own seat. "The doctors know what they're doing. If he listens I'm sure he'll be home with a private nurse by the end of the week."

Which meant Robert would be in the hospital for at

least two weeks, and probably cause at least three nurses to take mental health leave. Cade didn't care.

Now that he knew the old man would live, he'd done his duty by coming home. Now to get the hell out of here.

"He's going to be horribly bored," Catherine mused, as if terrorizing nurses and browbeating doctors wasn't entertainment enough for her son. "Maybe you could go by and visit this afternoon?"

"I don't think my visits are that good for his health," Cade said, offering a teasing smile to balance the bitterness in his words. As much as he loved his grandmother, he didn't see any point in perpetuating her naive hope that someday, somehow, her son and grandson would bond.

"It's good for both of you to spend time together," Catherine insisted, taking a dainty bite of her cookie before dipping the shortbread in her tea. "And it's a relief for him to know you're handling those little business issues."

"One issue, which is his trying to evict a neighbor you used to have over for teddy-bear tea parties," Cade pointed out. "And I haven't done anything to handle it so far."

"But you will, won't you?" Catherine leaned forward, her eyes intent as she gave her grandson the harshest look in her arsenal. The one that shot guilt like a laser. "Whatever your feelings about your father's business practices, Eden needs your help. You're going to help her figure out a way out of this, aren't you? Take care of her, please."

He'd taken damned good care of her last night.

But that was definitely not the kind of care his grandmother was talking about. Nor was it the kind he should even be thinking about, let alone wanting to repeat a few dozen times. He needed to forget about it. Pretend it had never happened.

Before he did something stupid.

"Mrs. Sullivan," Dora called from the door. "There's a phone call."

The live-in housekeeper offered Cade a friendly smile, but didn't give any other indication that she spoke to him on a monthly basis with updates on Catherine's well-being. If grandmother knew he was checking up on her, she'd pitch a fit. She'd probably follow it up with a hug and a plate of cookies, but Cade figured it was better to keep her fits to a minimum.

"Probably another person wanting to know all about your tête-à-tête with Eden last night. For someone who hasn't handled things, you've sure started a lot of chitchat around town," Catherine said, rising with an ease that belied her years. Her green eyes, so like Cade's own, twinkled behind round spectacles. "When I come back you can give me the details so I know what to tell people. And then you can fill me in on what really happened."

Holy hell.

And he was worried about doing something stupid?

He'd pretty much already covered that.

Cade managed to wait until his grandmother was out of the room before he buried his face in his hands and groaned.

God, what had he been thinking, going down on Eden like that?

Yes, she was fun and sexy and cute.

She was also a tie to the hometown he couldn't walk away from as long as his grandmother was alive. A tie that came with expectations. Responsibilities. Serious repercussions.

None of which Cade was willing to take on.

But, oh, God, she was delicious.

His mouth watering at the memory, Cade jumped to his feet.

Crazy. This was why ignoring his own rules was emotional suicide. Why getting involved with a friend was insane.

Unable to stay still, he paced the room. He scooped up a handful of cookies off the gilt-edged plate, tossing them, one at a time, in his mouth. Like always, he felt as if he was tiptoeing through a child's dollhouse here. Dainty furniture, gilt and crystal decorations. The surfaces were scattered with fresh flowers in everything from Baccarat to a mason jar, the bright scent of spring filling the air.

He wanted to leave. To get back to…what?

The base in Coronado?

What did it say about him that he had no interest in returning to the one place he really considered home?

Tension did a little tap dance along the back of his neck as Cade wondered what had happened.

He'd always been itching for another mission, amped up to dive into action.

Now?

Now he had nothing.

No enthusiasm.

No energy.

No interest.

Not in his career.

Definitely not in being back in his hometown.

The only thing that'd sparked any excitement was Eden, and she was off-limits. He'd stepped over the line, lost his head the night before. He was smart enough, savvy enough, to make sure it didn't happen again.

No matter how much he wanted it to.

One thing he could thank his father for, the old man had taught him young that you didn't always get what you wanted.

Tossing another cookie in his mouth, Cade stopped at

the grand piano. He hated that thing. It'd taken him a year to get out of the mandatory lessons his mother had insisted on. And at the tender age of six, the instrument had prompted his father to call him a quitter for the first time.

Good times.

His gaze skimmed the photos. Eighty years, plus, of framed memories scattered, dust-free, over the glossy black surface. His father's baby pictures, a variety of weddings, his own life in photos.

His eyes landed on an ebony frame. It was like a punch to the gut. Grinding his teeth, it took all his effort not to grab the photo and toss it out the window.

It was a photo of Cade, Blake Landon and Phil Hawkins on the day they'd graduated basic training. He used to laugh when he saw it. They were the epitome of the Three Amigos—Blake's uniform was perfectly pressed and his expression indulgent, Cade wore his dark shades looking like he was posing for a military ad, and Phil was cutting up by doing his Popeye impression. *Boy Scout, Slick* and *The Joker*.

They'd each earned—and lived up to—their nicknames.

Right up until one of them had died.

Cade's guts knotted, emotions wrapping around and getting them in a stranglehold.

It wasn't like he thought they were invincible. He'd always known the risks, reveled in them actually. They all had. And it wasn't like his belief in what they fought for, in their mission, had slipped any. He was still one-hundred percent on board.

But he was tired, dammit.

It felt like he'd been fighting, full-tilt, since he was a kid. First to get into the navy, then into the SEALs. Then, well, his job was to fight. Because he was damned good at it, he got to do it a lot.

Now?

Now he wondered how much fight he had left in him.

How long he could keep pushing before he hit the wall, burned out. Made a fatal mistake.

Cade hated that thought. Hated himself for entertaining it. He was grateful beyond words that his grandmother chose that moment to return. He almost grabbed her for a tight hug, so happy for the distraction from his miserable thoughts.

"That was Reba Carmichael. We're having lunch tomorrow to chat." Cade waited for his grandmother to take her seat before dropping into his own. "She said she has news, plus she wants me to see how much her cat has grown. I understand you met her yesterday?"

It took Cade a few seconds to shift his thoughts. Then another few to shove the lingering misery aside. He'd given up on eradicating it.

"Mrs. Carmichael?" he finally said. "I think I met her when I was in first grade."

"The cat, dear."

Oh. Cade replayed his grandmother's words.

"The cat Eden rescued?" At Catherine's nod, Cade shrugged. "Yeah, I guess so."

"That dear Eden. Reba said the sweet girl charmed her cat, who isn't easy to impress, truth be told. And incidentally why don't you tell me what you were doing with that sweet Gillespie girl last night if you weren't discussing your father's loan?" Catherine asked, watching him over the rim as she sipped her tea. There was a calculating look in those eyes, rarely seen, that clued Cade in to where his father had got some of his shrewd sense.

"You know, you're pretty lethal." Cade laughed drily. At his grandmother's chiding look, he gave a jerk of his shoulder. "It was just drinks. We never actually got around to talking about anything substantial because the town gossips kept stopping by and interrupting. I finally gave up and took her home."

With one short, incredibly delicious break between the bar and her house.

Not thinking about it in front of your grandmother, he scolded his body.

"But you'll help Eden before you leave, won't you? Make sure all this silly loan business is taken care of so she doesn't have to worry about her home?" Catherine prodded like a white-haired, velvet-covered steamroller. "She can't be made to pay for her mother's carelessness. That just wouldn't be fair, dear."

Why didn't she just tell her son to get off Eden's back? She had as much, no more, influence in this situation as Cade had. If it had been anyone else, he would have snapped. But this was his grandmother. For whatever reason, she never directly forced her son's hand. But she clearly wanted—with good reason—the threat to Eden's well-being dealt with.

How could he deny her that? Cade took a deep breath, leaned forward to pick up the cookie plate and offered it, and his most amiable smile.

"For you, Grandmother, anything," he promised.

His reward was a tittering laugh, a flutter of the lashes and his grandmother waving the last cookie toward him.

Yep, he thought as he bit into the buttery treat, charm always won out in the end.

"Now tell me, when are you going back to San Diego?" Catherine asked, those shrewd eyes still locked on him. "You've some decisions to make once you get there, don't you?"

Cade had to swallow the cookie crumbs that had just turned to dust in his throat before he could answer. What the hell? Did he have a sign over his head, proclaiming that his life was going down the toilet?

"Not as many as you'd think," he sidestepped. "I follow orders. That tends to take a lot of the decision making off my shoulders."

"But some things aren't ordered from higher up, are they?"

Like what to do with his career?

Or how to overcome the gut-wrenching feeling that he was betraying his own self by wanting a break from playing hero?

Then, a thought occurring to him, Cade narrowed his eyes and leaned forward to prop both elbows on his knees. He gave his grandmother a chiding look.

"You've been gossiping with Uncle Seth again, haven't you?"

"Don't be silly." As if her cheeks hadn't just turned bright pink, she tut-tutted before hiding behind her teacup again.

"So you're saying that Uncle Seth didn't call and talk to you about some possible changes in my MOS?"

"MOS, dear?"

Cade's smile widened. Oh, she was so good. He knew perfectly well that she knew more about military designations and terminology than most. But he knew the game, and how much she liked playing it.

"Military Occupational Specialty," he supplied, crossing one leg over the other and settling into the chair. "You know, job title."

"Oh, that MOS. I actually hadn't talked to Seth since the end of January. He calls every other month or so to keep me up to date on things." She gave a regretful look at her empty teacup, then set it down with a delicate snap before arching one elegant brow. "So, what would your uncle have told me about you changing jobs if he'd broken tradition and called early?"

Cade shook his head. Nope, not going there. The last thing he needed was more people weighing in on his career and trying to tell him what they thought he should do.

"If you weren't asking about my assignment, what were you referring to?"

"I had a lovely note from your friend, Blake."

What the hell? Blake was ratting him out now? Other than curling his hands into fists, Cade didn't show any reaction. But the minute he got a hold of his best friend...? His fingers throbbed.

"So...Blake wanted to inform you of, what? My current job performance evaluation? Isn't that a little above his pay grade?"

Not that it mattered that Blake was a Lieutenant and he was a Lieutenant Commander. Cade had never saw the rank difference as more than a couple of training choices, since Blake had spent two years focused on linguistics while Cade played with guns.

But still, where did the guy get off talking shit to Cade's grandmother? Wasn't he supposed to be a friend? What happened to covering each other's asses?

Catherine gave him a long, considering look before getting to her feet, crossing over to where he sat and grabbing the cookie out of his hand.

"Bratty mouths don't deserve sweets," she said primly. With enough force to turn the treat to crumbs, she smacked the cookie on the plate, then sat back down like nothing had happened.

Cade stared at his grandmother, then at the plate.

Damn. Regretting more than the loss of his snack, he sighed.

"I'm sorry," Cade said honestly. "Why don't you tell me what Blake was contacting you about."

Because it hadn't been about Cade, his job or anything personal. Blake didn't do that. The guy took his commitments—and friendship was a major one—as seriously as his missions.

"His lovely fiancée sent an engagement announcement, and I replied. We know her family, after all. She mentioned that Blake would be having you stand as his best man. So I, of course, contacted him directly to offer my congratulations."

"Oh."

Best man. Cade shifted, trying to adjust the fit of his shirt as it suddenly seemed to be squeezing his shoulders. Why was Blake even thinking about getting married? The guy was crazy.

"Oh, indeed. Now you can go brew me more tea while you consider why you are so surly."

Surly?

Cade bit back the response, offering a genial smile and nod instead and taking the teacup and empty-except-for-his-confiscated-crumbs cookie plate with him to the kitchen.

He didn't need the five minutes it took to boil water and pour it over a pile of dried flowers to know what had him on edge.

Everything was wrong. His edgy, exciting life—the one he'd dreamed of and planned for and, dammit, loved—just wasn't anymore.

Wasn't exciting.

Wasn't what he'd dreamed.

Wasn't what he loved.

Everything had changed.

Now Blake was changing, too. Getting married, for

God's sake. Why? Sure, Alexia was hot. Funny and smart and perfect for the Boy Scout. But it wasn't like she was holding out for a ring. Maybe it was because her father was an admiral, and could make Blake's life hell.

That had to be it. Why else would a guy, a SEAL, put himself or anyone else through the insanity that went hand in hand with being married to special ops?

There. That's why he was surly.

Because his life was off track, out of whack and his best friend was making a huge mistake.

Nothing a little time wouldn't fix.

Then he glanced out his grandmother's kitchen window.

Eden.

This wasn't surly he was fighting.

It was horny.

Even from this distance, the sight of her lithe body sent a wakeup call to his libido.

He warned his body to stand down. Talk about marriage material. Eden practically had "I Do" stamped over her head. Not because she seemed like she was interested in the wedding ordeal. But because the town would expect it. His grandmother, if she thought there was something between him and Eden, would totter right out to her greenhouse and start gathering lilies for the ceremony.

He winced when the goat butted Eden, using enough force to send her sideways. Surprisingly, for a girl prone to accidents, she didn't lose her footing. Instead, she turned and threw her arms around the goat's neck for a hug. She was too far away to hear but Cade could imagine her gurgling laughter as she played with the animals.

Damn, she was something.

He sighed.

If he left before the loan was settled for his father, Robert would start foreclosure action faster than the bank.

Eden would lose everything. And Catherine would smack him upside the head.

If he stuck around, he didn't think he could resist Eden. Not for long. Not after tasting her. Feeling her. Hearing the noises she made when she came, saw how she responded to sex. How would she look when he got her completely naked? Would she be as demanding and assertive when she touched him as she had been with herself?

What did her nipples taste like? How did it feel to slide inside her body? Did she like it on top? On bottom?

She bent over to scoop up the dogs' ball.

He groaned.

Did she like it from behind?

Realizing he was hard and horny in his grandmother's kitchen, Cade groaned and forced himself to turn away from the window.

Tea. Cookies. Torture.

He had to get the hell out of here.

Unable to resist, he looked at Eden again. The dogs romped while she watched, one arm draped affectionately over the goat.

And maybe he'd just figured out how to escape.

Knowing better than to get cocky, because plans had a way of being shot to hell, Cade still felt pretty confident when he strode into the sitting room.

"Grandmother," he asked, offering her tea and a fresh plate of shortbread. "Have you ever considered getting a pet?"

9

MY, HOW THINGS COULD CHANGE in just a few days. Pretending she wasn't a little shell-shocked—and pessimistically positive it wouldn't last—Eden circulated between clients in the clinic lobby, taking a payment from one and offering another's puppy a treat while telling the third she'd be right with him.

Five days ago, right after her night with Cade, dozens of people had come in to get the inside dirt on their date. When they'd realized she wasn't giving anything away free, the smart ones had made appointments for their pets. For the price of a checkup here, an inoculation there and the occasional heartworm test, they'd gotten damned good veterinary service to go with the coy responses Eden had liberally dished around.

She'd been delighted when she'd tallied her receipts from all those nosy new clients. Given that the bank manager was an old family friend, and the fact that Eden hadn't known anything about the loan, he'd agreed to accept a one-time payment against the interest, and extend the loan another thirty days. So she had a month to get her mother home to deal with it—or to find thirty grand to pay it off herself.

"Eden, I want to make an appointment for next week. You'll be around, won't you? Not jetting off somewhere with Cade?"

Eden's smile was a little shaky around the edges as she assured the woman she was taking appointments all month. Hurt tangled with disappointment, but she wasn't about to confess that she hadn't seen or heard from her hot, sexy date since Cade had dropped her at her front door.

"Thanks so much for bringing the kitten in for a visit," she said to the next client as she handed her the invoice. "If you decide to go ahead and get her vaccinated, let me know."

Eden had to resist the urge to shake her head. The woman had obviously already had her cat to a different vet, gotten a thorough checkup and all the accompanying care. But, hey, everyone knew by now that Eden wasn't offering info for free.

"Mrs. Went, would you like to bring your goldfish back now? We'll see if we can figure out why she's swimming slower than normal," she offered, keeping her smile in place. If they wanted to pay for her to meet their pets, that was on them. And maybe one or two would be impressed enough to make the next visit real.

Eden figured she'd be ready for her Pollyanna tattoo before the weekend.

Two hours later, her feet were hurting, her smile wilting and her mood edgy. She watched the last customer leave for the day, then hauled out the mop and cleanser. Maybe she should offer housebreaking classes. At least then her new clients would go away with something other than frustration.

She wondered what it said about her that she was so happy to share that particular feeling, even if she wasn't sharing any gossipy news.

Because *she* was frustrated. And angry. And feeling like a damned fool.

What had she been thinking, trying to seduce Cade Sullivan?

Now, instead of a buddy, the sexy guy who fueled her fantasies and hauled her out of trees, he was *that guy*.

The one she'd gone too far with. Not physically. That particular experience hadn't gone nearly far enough. But she'd gone too far counting on him. Actually thinking he'd finish the bone-melting job he'd started. That he'd be interested enough after a taste to come back for the whole banquet.

Instead, he'd pulled a dine and dash.

According to his grandmother, if the ever-so-reliable gossip that'd kept her doors open the last few days was to be trusted, Cade was only gone for a few days.

According to the miserable knot that was now living in Eden's stomach, everything was ruined.

Her easy, comfortable relationship with Cade.

The pride she took in just being herself, and pretending that she didn't care if people accepted that or not.

And her secretly cherished fantasy that after one kiss, he would be so crazy for her that he wouldn't be able to resist showing her every sort of delight she'd heard he had to offer.

She slammed the mop into the sink and smacked the knob to send water spraying everywhere.

She blamed Cade, she decided as she quickly adjusted the flow. She really did.

If only because he made her think she could have everything she'd dreamed of.

Before she could slide into the pout that had become her almost-constant companion over the last day or so, the phone rang. Turning off the water, she hurried across the room.

"Gillespie," she answered.

"Eden, how's business?"

Bev's good cheer floated across the line like music, upbeat and chipper.

And totally irritating.

"Booming, thanks to the gossip ghouls," Eden snapped. Then, like a geyser, all her frustration came spouting to the surface, casting a verbal splatter all over the place. "What is with these people? It's bad enough that they think they can bullshit their way into getting me to unwittingly spill information. It's another to be so blatant about it that it becomes an insult to both me and to themselves. You'd think they'd care enough to at least try to be clever with their snooping."

Bev's laugh rang over the telephone line, doing more to ease Eden's frustration than any coddling commiseration could have.

"Well, as lousy as they are, I've given three perms, touched up two color jobs that are so fresh I can still smell the toner and given six kids their first haircut."

"Pumping you for information, too?" Eden leaned against the counter and shook her head before giving in to the laughter. "That's just sad."

"At least we're making money out of it."

"I wonder if we can drag this out for another two months," Eden muttered, figuring it'd take that long at her current rate of would-be clients to pay off the bank loan. Especially if the bank manager charged her the seventeen-percent he'd mumbled about when they'd made their appointment.

Before Bev could offer encouragement, or some wild

new idea to capitalize on this newfound popularity, the front door opened.

Damn.

"I've got to go," Eden murmured, not waiting for her friend to disconnect. As she always did when faced with the Oceanfront girls, Eden wished for a mirror. Silly wish, since there wasn't much she could do to fancy up a ponytail, jeans and purple T-shirt.

"Hey there," she greeted Janie and Crystal as they stepped into the converted barn as gingerly as if the linoleum floor were covered with horse droppings. "I'm sorry, but I closed about a half hour ago. Unless you were here to make an appointment?"

Since neither woman had a pet, she didn't figure that was the case.

"Oh, no. We just stopped by to visit," Janie said, sniffing surreptitiously before letting the door close behind her and coming into the center of the lobby to look around in fascinated curiosity.

Poor thing, she obviously didn't get to go slumming very often.

Eden had to give them credit, though. Unlike the townspeople, and a few of the other Oceanfront set, at least they didn't bother with subterfuge.

"Visit?" she prompted, since they'd never, in all their years of growing up together, sought her out before. "Really?"

"We're here about the Spring Fling," Crystal said, walking over to the cat cage where three kittens were snoozing after a busy day of chasing visiting pets. "It's going to be so fun. And the dresses this year are to die for. You're going, aren't you?"

The cats woke, one of them pouncing on Crystal's finger like it was a toy mouse. Eden waited for the woman to complain, but instead she giggled and reached between the cage bars to rub the furry ears.

"I haven't missed a year yet." Wondering if she'd misjudged Crystal, Eden walked over to unlatch the cage. The cats scrambled out to climb all over the pretty blonde, who laughed with delight. "Why would this one be any different?"

"Well, you haven't brought a date in a lot of years, either," Janie said, her smile brightly cheerful. "So we wanted to offer to help you this year."

"To help me…? What? Get a date?"

Both women giggled like she'd just recited a naughty limerick.

There once was a girl on a rock
Who developed an intense craving for Cade's—

"Of course not," Janie said with a wave of her Kate Spade purse. "I'm sure you've got that covered. I mean, I know it's been a few years since you broke Kenny's foot the weekend before the dance, but it's not like anyone's keeping track to see who you bring."

"Or who brings me?"

They wanted to know if she was going to the big country club party with Cade. The knot in Eden's stomach tightened, making her a little ill.

"So why were you here again? Just to do a party head-count?"

"Oh, no, we're not on the RSVP committee," Crystal said, holding two cats now, her face buried in their fur. "We're on the decorating committee."

"We're driving down to San Francisco tomorrow," Janie explained, her tone upbeat and suspiciously friendly. "You know, shopping, lunch, fun stuff like that. We thought you might like to go."

Once upon a time…heck, was it only a month ago, she'd

have done anything for that kind of invitation. To be asked to join their exclusive little world. To be accepted, even on the fringes.

Now it held about as much appeal as being shaved bald and forced at gunpoint to sing "Achy Breaky Heart" while break dancing.

Because even if they did accept her, the minute they realized Cade was out of the picture and Eden wasn't great gossip fodder any longer, they'd push her right back out.

Smiling, so she wouldn't give in to the stupid tears burning her eyes, she crossed both arms over her chest and arched one brow. "Because, what? You think I need to be decorated?"

"Of course not. You have wonderful taste in clothes," Janie said in a humor-the-deluded tone. "We just thought it'd be fun for you. You know, maybe even throw in a makeover, and if you wanted, some lingerie shopping."

Oh, nicely done. Eden barely kept her sarcastic applause to herself.

The backhanded-insult attempt to garner information. She wished she could tell them that she didn't need lingerie, because Cade liked her better naked. That'd wipe the smirks off their faces so fast, they wouldn't be able to smile for a week.

"Ladies."

Eden jumped, her heart pounding at the sudden pivot from anger to surprise. She hadn't heard anyone come in. From Janie and Crystal's expressions, they hadn't, either.

While the other women made a show of girly excitement, complete with hands waving in front of their faces and one grabbing the counter as if to keep from falling, Eden eyed Cade, then the door. He must have caught the bell before it could chime. Extensive special-ops training for sneaking up on gossiping women, no doubt.

All three of them moved toward the center of the lobby to meet Cade, but unlike the other two, Eden didn't giggle, twitter or preen. Nor did she greet him with a smile.

Why would she? He'd brought her to a screaming orgasm, patted her on the head and disappeared.

Like he'd heard she'd been in a sexual drought and figured that was the next area of her life he'd sweep in and save.

And now that she was under mean-girl siege, he just happened to show up? Did he have an Eden's-up-the-creek beeper or something?

"Playing hero again?" she murmured with a scowl.

Neither Janie nor Crystal gave any sign of having heard her. Cade did, though. He arched a brown and shot her a wicked, *what else were you expecting* sort of look.

Eden didn't know what she had been expecting.

She just knew that she'd given up on expecting *him*.

CADE HATED BULLIES.

Even when those bullies were women. More so, he realized, since the female persuasion seemed to take an extra catty delight in knowing exactly where to stick the knife.

He didn't know what they'd been giving Eden crap about—he was just glad he would step in and stop it. He hadn't expected it to be quite this easy, though. Instead of doubling down on their bullying, they'd both plastered on friendly, there's-nothing-to-see-here innocent expressions before offering bubbling, friendly greetings.

Eden didn't look quite so thrilled.

As a matter of fact, he'd never seen her look quite as unthrilled to see him. Instead of the usual mischievously welcoming smile he was used to being greeted with, she just stared.

Cade twitched his shoulders, trying to throw off the feeling of guilt that was trying to settle there.

What? He hadn't made any promises. Oral sex on a rock under the moonlight wasn't a binding commitment, dammit. And he'd had to get away. The drive down the coast to San Francisco, a couple of days with Blake and Alexia—he'd needed that to clear his head after...

After losing it to the taste of Eden. After getting so tied up in worrying about her expectations that he'd essentially done the one thing he hated, the one his father always liked to toss out. He'd run away.

Still, he'd come back.

And if the crap she was taking was any indication, he'd arrived just in time.

"Cade," the tall woman said, tottering over with less grace than Eden had shown at the cliffs wearing crazy heels. Batting her lashes like they'd help her balance, she squeezed his arm and pressed her boobs against his shoulder in greeting. "Welcome home. I haven't seen you yet to tell you how sorry we were to hear about your father."

We? Was she wearing a crown?

"He's not dead," Cade said, shrugging off her comment and her hold on him.

"But he had a horrible heart attack. Triple bypass—that had to be scary."

"You're talking to a guy who faces down automatic weapons, live grenades and sings cadence with a bunch of guys," Eden said dryly. "I think he sees scary in a slightly different way than you do."

"Oh, Eden," the taller woman said, shaking her head and looking to Cade as if for sympathy. Why, he had no idea. "I'm sure he's been frantic with worry, which is just like fear, isn't it? Your poor father. The Garden Club ladies were at the hospital just this morning to check on him. You must be so glad he'll be home tomorrow."

Since his gramma would smack him for saying otherwise, Cade kept his response behind closed lips.

He looked back at Eden, wondering how she managed to look so much better, fresher, sexier than the two dolled-up tarts standing next to her.

He'd missed her.

He shouldn't have.

He never missed people. Not from his hometown, none of his friends, not even his family. Hell, he didn't even miss Phil, but that was probably because he refused to let himself think about his old buddy.

But he'd missed Eden.

Missed her smile, her laughter, and the sweet sexy scent of honeysuckle that seemed to float around her like a soft cloud.

He'd missed the taste of her.

How could a guy become addicted after just one small taste? And once hooked, how did he get over her without tearing up both of their lives?

"Hey, Eden," he greeted, his tone low, and probably a little friendlier than she wanted, given the audience.

"Cade."

Hmm, maybe that missing had been one-sided?

"Sorry I was gone so long."

He'd had to remove himself from temptation, sure if he'd stuck around, he'd have done something crazy. Like beg Eden to sleep with him.

But the minute he'd gotten back into town, he hadn't been able to resist coming to see her. And so far, so good. No begging yet.

"We were just talking about the Spring Fling," the tall woman interrupted. What the hell was her name? He tried to remember it as she did that lash-fluttering thing again. She must be hell on wheels during allergy season. "All the girls are wondering if this is the year you'll finally bring a date. A real one, not just your grandmother."

Subtle. Cade looked at Eden, whose eyes were dancing with delight. At his expense, no less.

"I'm not really into the country club events," Cade side-stepped.

Not far enough, though.

"Oh, this isn't just any event. You probably know your grandmother is hosting this year, and dedicating the auction funds to her veterans' program. She must be thrilled you're home, since your presence alone will guarantee people bid even more."

Well. Guilt, served up with a side of eyelash fluttering. He wasn't buying it, though. Still, afraid she'd grab his arm again, Cade shifted away, heading toward Eden. Not safety, he wasn't stupid. He knew damned well she was the most dangerous person in this building. But her kind of danger, he wouldn't mind sampling a few more times.

"You're going, aren't you?" the blonde prodded.

Cade debated. He didn't want to go, but he knew the power of a good show. If he put one on, he might have a better chance of manipulating his father into cutting a deal over the loan. And if the rumors he'd been hearing since getting back that morning were anything to go by, his going would likely toss a whole lot more business Eden's way. A win-win.

"Yeah, I'm going," he said. Then, tired of their snotty-ass attitudes toward Eden, he fully committed to the danger zone and stepped over, wrapping his arm around Eden's shoulders. He had to hold on extra tight when she almost jumped across the room.

Amping up his smile to keep the two barracudas' attention on himself, he added, "With Eden."

IT WAS LIKE BEING WRAPPED in a warm blanket of sexually charged delight and facing a barrage of poison arrows at the same time.

Eden didn't know whether to sigh in pleasure, or duck and run. Given the fury in Janie's pretty blue eyes, running wouldn't matter. The other woman was going to catch up sooner or later.

So, what was a girl to do?

Figuring spite over his disappearance wasn't worth keeping herself from enjoying whatever game he was playing, Eden leaned into his body, absorbing the warm, solid comfort he offered. She wasn't sure where the comfort came from. Maybe her usual, sexually overloaded reaction was inhibited by the women glaring at them. Hard to be horny when the voyeurs wanted to scratch your face off.

"You're taking Eden to the Spring Fling?" Janie asked in the same tone one would use to humor a two-year-old who'd just claimed they were going to fly to the moon on their teddy bear.

"And me, with nothing special to wear," Eden deadpanned, thrilled to throw Janie's words back at her.

Cade leaned closer, his breath tickling her ear as he whispered, "Something that goes with that red bra would be nice."

Despite her irritation over his disappearance, Eden gurgled with laughter and slanted him a naughty look.

"How interesting," Janie snapped, tucking her purse under her arm and grabbing Crystal with her other hand. "I guess we'll just have to do that shopping trip without you, Eden. See you at the ball."

With that, a chilly look and a tug on her stunned friend's arm, Janie glided out like she was floating on ice.

"Aww, I think you upset them," Eden said, still laughing as the front door slammed shut. "It's going to be painful, given that they came in for gossip and you sent them off with the best of the season. But Janie's going to have to choose between spreading the word or being pissed that you're claiming to take me to the social event of the season."

"Claim? I don't lie." At her doubtful look, Cade frowned. "Why wouldn't I take you?"

Easing out from under his arm so as to reboot the circuit to her brain, Eden rolled her eyes.

"Why wouldn't you take me, in their opinion? Or in reality?"

She blinked a couple times at the flash of fury in his eyes, but before she could do more than bite her lip, it was gone.

"Let's get their opinion out of the way, since it seems to matter to you."

"Oh, no," she exclaimed wide-eyed, giving a dismissive wave of her hand as if she could as easily shoo away the truth. "I don't care what they think. Although this will put an interesting spin on the *Who's Cade With Now* chitchat."

She could imagine the shock, dismay and questions. Drinks at the Wayfarers were one thing. Bringing the equivalent of a poor relation to the biggest social event of the year? That was like stepping up to pitch in the gossip major leagues.

"You have a problem with your name being linked to mine?"

Eden's lips twitched, wondering if he knew he sounded like a pouty ten-year-old.

"It sounds like you're the one worried about gossip,"

she said, gathering up the kittens and putting them back in their cage. Then she went to the supply closet to finish up her closing cleaning routine. "And their reasons are three-fold. I'm not wealthy. I might break something of yours they're going to want to use if you date them. And taking me means you're not taking one of them."

There. Three simple reasons, presented in her best non-whiny fashion.

"And what about you?"

"Me?" she asked, glancing up from her task of cleaning one of the cat boxes. "I'm closer to poor than non-wealthy. I never try to break things—it just happens. And I'm sure the perception that you already have a date will keep them from dogging you in hopes of getting asked out."

When he didn't respond, she finished the last cat box, then made her way through the lobby, reception area and exam room to empty trash bins. She returned two minutes later to find him still standing in the center of the room, arms crossed over his chest and a grumpy frown on his face.

"Do you have an excuse lined up?" she asked, hoping they were good ones. She'd realized that being blown off after starring in the *How'd She Get Him To Do That* gossip was going to be quite a slap. "Will you say you were called back to duty? An overseas emergency?"

"What are you talking about?"

Leaving the garbage bag by the door, she pushed a stray hair behind her ear and gave him a chiding look. "Well you're not really going to the Spring Fling with me, and I can't not go because I promised your grandmother I'd help out. So what excuse are you going to give?"

"I'm going with you," he insisted.

"Oh, please, you are not. You just said that because Janie was being a brat. That was a typical Cade Sullivan rescue."

His frown turned deadly.

Eden tried to swallow, but the look in his eyes dried up her throat.

Wow.

She'd always thought of Cade as a charmer, an easygoing guy who looked sexy as hell in a navy uniform. But she rarely thought of him as military. Until the other night when he'd mentioned losing his friend, she'd never thought of him as a fighter.

But that look, the one right there on his face?

That twisted her perception all around.

And made her shiver with apprehension. He wasn't just the boy next door. There were depths there, things he'd done, things he could do, that were beyond her ability to relate to. He wasn't just the guy she'd always crushed on now.

Now, he was a dangerous man who was suddenly way more than she could safely handle.

"A typical rescue?" he repeated, his words low, with a cold edge. Like he was seeing her in a whole different light, too.

Eden didn't care. She couldn't, wouldn't, pretend to be something she wasn't. Which included being meek and sweet just to get her forever crush to like her. Dammit, she wasn't in eighth grade and this wasn't child's play. Even if it did include an end-of-season dance.

"Of course this is another Cade Sullivan rescue. You've never attended the Spring Fling with a date, and nothing you say will convince me that you wanted to this year. The only reason you said you were taking me was to get Janie and Crystal to back off," she dismissed, irritated that her words came out shaky and hoping he'd take that as nerves instead of hurt.

"That wasn't bullshit," he denied. "I want to take you to the party."

Her heart leaped, excited and hopeful. She stomped it down quickly, since the defensive tone and quick flash of regret on his face didn't scream *happy date* to her.

"Why?" she asked, suddenly tired of being his pet project. Someone only worthy of his attention if she needed rescuing. Well, dammit, she was tired of having him see her as a mission. If he couldn't want her as a woman— a desirable, strong, worthy-of-him woman—she wished he'd just leave.

Again.

"Why?" he repeated, frustration and anger clear on his face.

"Yes," she challenged, lifting her palms to the air. "Why."

Cade's jaw worked, emotions chasing too fast through his eyes for her to keep up. Then, clearly reaching a conclusion—one that looked like it was going to scare the hell out of her, if that dark look was any indication—he stomped over.

"What—"

Before she could finish asking what he was doing, he grabbed both her arms and lifted her off her feet. Pulling her body tight against his, he bent low.

"This is why," he told her just before he took her mouth.

Eden melted, sinking into the kiss with a low moan.

He was so yummy.

And he wanted her.

That cautious—and totally inconvenient—little voice screamed out a warning. He was out of her league. So far out that she didn't have the first comprehension of what his real life was like. Four days ago, he'd been her hero. The boy next door who always pulled her out of the tree. But he was bigger and sexier and scarier and more intense now.

Slowly, reluctantly, she forced herself to pull away from

the most delicious kiss of her life. She barely held back a
protesting whimper.

Her lashes fluttered as she made herself meet his gaze.
His green eyes were like lasers, looking past her soul and
into that corner where her fears hid. He saw everything,
could do anything.

She slid out of his arms before she could curl up closer
and beg for another taste.

She wanted him.

And she was desperately afraid she was falling in love
with him.

10

"WELL," EDEN SAID, breathless as she pressed her fingers to her lips, looking like he'd just shocked her all to hell and back. "That's a good reason for a lot of things. But are you sure you want to do them in public? Because there's nothing more public than this event."

Hands fisted in his pockets so he wouldn't grab her again, Cade paced to the window to glare at the overgrown paddock.

What the hell was he doing? He'd wanted to see her, yes. But his reasons for coming here were much more practical. He needed to fill her in on the loan his father was trying to collect from her mother. And he wanted to arrange for her to get a pet for his grandmother. Next thing he knew, he was throwing out public declarations and playing grab-ass like a desperate sailor on his first leave.

He'd lived within specific protocols long enough to know he was stepping way over the line. There were times you took one for the squad, you risked it all for the mission. And then there was going so far off the deep end that you were practically AWOL. Doing this? Going after Eden? That was the equivalent of going rogue.

He knew what he was supposed to do.

He'd spent four days solidifying his mission plan and choices, outlining the known factors, considering the options and detailing his escape routes.

The mission was to get out of Ocean Point with everything the same as when he'd arrived. Which meant no crazy commitments, no broken hearts, no emotional drama.

The choices had been simple. Give in to his desire for Eden. Or do some damage control, convincing her that nothing had changed between them.

Known factors?

Eden was the girl he rescued, and even though she didn't know it, she currently needed his help.

She was tied to Ocean Point, and would have to face the gossips and innuendos long after he left.

She was deliciously sweet, in more ways than one.

She was fun and cute and made him feel like he could leap, fly and save the world.

If it wasn't for his dedication to the military, to his career as a SEAL, she was the kind of girl he'd want to settle down with. Which made her about as dangerous as a mountain of explosives in a lightning storm.

So her pushing him away?

It was the best thing she could have done for both of their sakes.

"Are you saying you don't want to go to the party with me?" he asked, totally aware as the words left his lips that he'd crossed the line.

"I'm just saying that I don't think it's a really good idea," she told him, her words slow and careful, as if she were measuring each one before she let it cross her tongue. "It's not like it's two buddies going out for a drink, you know? If we went to this event—because the dance isn't just another country club party—we'd be making a statement."

"You mean the gossips will go crazy talking about us, making up all kinds of stuff and trying to outdo each other with their brilliantly manufactured insider information?"

Eden's lips twitched and she rolled her eyes as if to say he was being ridiculous. Good. He was glad she could see how stupid it was to let other people factor into whether or not they went together.

"Exactly."

"Exactly, what?" Cade frowned. Was she agreeing with his gossip assessment? Or had she tapped into his thoughts and was reassuring him that she'd be totally on board with having a no-strings relationship with him in front of the entire town?

"The gossips would go crazy over the news that you were dating me. They already are, actually. It won't matter that it's a pity date thrown out in another of your routine rescues."

Cade wasn't sure which phrase sent his pissed meter through the roof. Pity date, or routine rescue. Both were pretty damned insulting.

"You think that's all there is between us? Pity rescues?"

She winced, then lifted her palms and gave him a sad look. "What else is there?"

He'd had it. He was so tired of denying his wants, turning away from his needs. He was sick of being the nice guy, dammit.

"What else is there? Do you need a reminder," he asked, giving in to the need to pull her close again. He took her lips before she could voice the protest he saw in her dark eyes. It only took a few seconds before passion blurred her gaze and she kissed him back.

He couldn't get enough of her.

His lips shifted, his mouth angling to take hers deeper. Why was this a bad idea again?

His need for her overruled everything.

Even his ability to think.

"Stop," she whispered, her mouth still moving against his.

"No."

His hands skimmed her hips, up her waist and cupped her breasts. He groaned, reveling in the wonder of her softness. Her fullness. He squeezed, loving how she filled his palms, making his body ache for more.

He angled his body closer, so his hardening length pressed tight against her hip. She moaned, soft and low, making his fingers tighten before he slipped one hand over the curve of her waist to tug the soft fabric of her T-shirt away from her jeans.

Before he could find flesh, though, her hand shot up and grabbed his wrist. Eden pulled her mouth away from his. Her eyes fluttered open and she stared for a second before giving a regretful moan. She brushed her lips against his, super-fast, then ripped herself from his arms to scurry a few feet away.

"I can't… Here… Um…" She shoved both hands through her hair, loosened now that he'd tossed her ponytail holder somewhere on the floor. "I work here."

"So? We can do other things here, too," he reasoned, reaching for her again. His fingers barely skimmed her waist before she skipped away.

"Nope. Not here," she said shaking her head. She didn't look like she wanted to stop, though. Her eyes were eating him up like candy, the heat in them enough to melt his shorts.

"Why not?" he finally demanded, wanting to hear her tell him to his face that she wasn't interested. Because her nipples were still saying the opposite as they pressed, hard and pebbled, against her T-shirt.

Before she could say anything, the front door opened. In came a handful of women, a gaggle of kids and, weirdly, the goat.

They all stopped, looks of shock and speculation chasing over their faces.

"Hey, Eden," one of the women greeted. A chorus of hellos followed. "We're here for the 4H meeting. Thanks again for letting us use the back room."

"Sure." Eden look flustered for a minute, then shook her head like she was tossing off a fog and gestured to a wide set of doors. "It's all set for your meeting. Just lock up when you leave."

The women slanted curious looks their way but didn't ask questions as they herded the kids toward the room. He did see one give another a hip bump and a giggle before glancing back and blushing.

Looked like another segment of Ocean Point had something to talk about now.

"When is this over?" Cade asked, wondering which would come first, talking himself out of sex with Eden, or exploding from pent-up frustration. If her meeting ran more than fifteen minutes, either one was distinctly possible.

"The 4H meeting?" Eden glanced back as one attendee led the goat into the room before looking at the clock. "They should wind up around four-thirty."

"They?"

"I'm not in the 4H," she said, her shrug a little wistful. Cade wondered why she wasn't, since she was totally into animals. Was it anything like why she wasn't a part of the Oceanfront snob patrol, even though she had the family pedigree to qualify?

"So you don't have to stay?"

"I usually don't."

The girl with the goat and the one with the wicked hip bump both stood in the doorway, pretending to inspect the dog food display. Cade was pretty sure they were tilting sideways, considering how close they were leaning to try and eavesdrop.

"Let's go," he suggested, wondering if it sounded like begging to everyone else in the room or if that was just in his head.

"Go?"

"Yeah," he said, grabbing her hand and pulling her toward the door. *"Go."*

"Where are we going?" Eden's nerves were jumping all over the place as excitement, fear and anticipation wound through her system. She wanted to show a little pride and pull away, proving she wasn't a pushover. That she wasn't going to let him give her another wildly intense, mind-blowing orgasm and then just waltz away without a word.

"Let's go somewhere private. Your place is close," he suggested with a wicked smile, his fingers twining through hers.

Eden glanced toward the house for a considering second before sliding her eyes to the cars parked in front of the barn-slash-veterinary-clinic-slash-4H-classroom.

The house was close. A little too close to the barn-slash-vet-clinic filled with kids and curious adults. Many of whom she was sure had their noses pressed against the window at that exact moment.

She couldn't deny that she'd enjoyed reaping the benefits of the gossips this week. Cade was better than an ad, a coupon and a social-media blitz all rolled into one. But maybe it was time for a little caution. Because it wasn't just her reputation on the line here.

She was horribly afraid it might be her heart, too.

"How about we walk?" she countered, unable to deny herself more time with him despite the risk. She gestured to the path that traversed between both their properties. "We can take the lakeside trail. It's always so pretty along there."

"You want to go to the lake?" he asked, his voice dropping. It wasn't until she saw the flash of heat in his green eyes that she remembered. If he hadn't been holding her hand, she'd have used it to smack herself in the forehead. The lake was his spot. Initiations, sexual escapades, good times. She knew that. She'd fantasized about it so many times that the suggestion must have popped out of her subconscious.

Eden clenched her teeth in case some of the butterflies in her stomach escaped. Here it was, her only birthday wish of the last handful of years, ready to come true. All she had to do was let it.

"You sure you want to revisit the lake?" he asked, his words teasing and low. So low that he had to lean closer, so his warm breath washed over her, to deliver them.

Had he seen her all those times? Did he know she used to watch him there? Nerves flickering, Eden licked her lips. She gave him a wide-eyed look, then glanced toward the woods before asking, "What's wrong with the lake?"

"You don't have very good luck there, do you?"

"I beg your pardon?" What? Was he the only one who got to get lucky at the lake?

"Two years ago, I had to rescue you there, remember? Kenny Phillips was rolling naked in a batch of poison oak, trying to scare you away from sex."

Well, there it was. Now Eden knew she *could* cringe and laugh at the same time.

"How do you know I didn't scare him away from sex?" she asked, saying aloud what was usually whispered behind her back. "Word is he's never been the same, performance-wise."

Cade shrugged, his hand tightening as he helped her climb over a large fallen log in the path. "I don't know what you saw in the guy, but from what I recall, Kenny never was what I'd call a go-getter. He was second string, junior varsity, class presidential runner-up. You know, the kind of guy who never could go all the way."

Eden pressed her lips together to keep from admitting that those comments could easily be applied to Kenny's lovemaking skills, as well. After all, she'd broken the guy's foot. It'd just be rude to add insult to injury, even two years after the fact.

"I can't believe you showed up when you did two years ago," she said instead, still wondering how that'd happened. She hadn't even known he was coming home, so it wasn't like she'd had her rendezvous there in a subconscious attempt to send him some sexually charged message. "What are the odds?"

"I'd say the odds were pretty good since you're my, what'd you call it? Routine rescue?"

Eden grimaced. She should have known he'd throw that back at her. But she couldn't deny it. And, if she was honest, she didn't really want to. It was kinda nice, having her own personal hero.

"I didn't mean for that to sound so dismissive," she said quietly, following the pressure of his hand as he pulled her off the path, through the overgrown—but poison oak free—grasses toward the remote lake. "I really do appreciate you being there to haul me out of trouble. Or to step in when it seems like someone's picking on me."

"You're talking about the Spring Fling?"

"It was a sweet gesture," she said earnestly. It really was. Even if it made her feel like crawling under a rock. Eden sighed. She just wished, just one damned time in her life, that someone could want her for her. Not for what they could get or out of obligation. "But it's only going to put you in an uncomfortable position. That's a lousy thank-you for all the help you've given me."

He grimaced. He looked like he was going to say something—agree or protest, she wasn't sure. But before he could, they stepped through the tight ring of trees to the clearing surrounding the lake.

Eden hummed in appreciation, a combination of sensual energy and relaxation wrapping around her like a sexually charged, but cozy, blanket. The setting was gorgeous. A serene blend of earth tones gave a gentle background to the mossy green water. Rocks as tall as her hip, rounded by years of weather, stood sentinel. Sunlight glinted through the overhead leaves, warming the cool glade with a soft glow.

"You're the one who was looking uncomfortable. The gossips are a pain but you don't have to let them bother you. Why do you deal with snobby chicks like that Janie?"

Because she kept hoping for acceptance. Belonging. History.

Since the first two sounded pathetic, she went with the third.

"My family helped found Ocean Point. On both my mom and my dad's side, they were integral to everything, from founding the library to creating laws. My great-grandfather actually donated the land the country club is built on. That all makes me a part of the Oceanfront set," she said. No need to add that because her family was broke, her father gone and her mother dancing on the crazy side of irresponsible, some of the set would happily ignore that history and let her fade into a footnote in the town ledger. Cade already knew all that.

"Why not just move away?"

Huh? Eden blinked a couple of times, trying to process the idea. "I can't leave Ocean Point."

"Why not?"

"Because this is my home."

He just arched one brow. Panic grappled and clawed its way through Eden's stomach. Her life might not be everything she wanted, but she'd always lived it here. She might not fit perfectly, but at least her rut was dug in and familiar.

"Every place has its games and rules and drawbacks," she said with a shrug. "But here, I know the players, I can work the rules and sidestep the drawbacks. But more importantly, there are things here worth doing all that for."

"Like?"

She narrowed her eyes, realizing he wasn't just being argumentative. He really didn't see the benefits of his home town.

"Like knowing everyone, having those ties that go back. Not just to kindergarten or T-ball. But all the way back, generations. Like the familiarity of the places. Knowing where to get steak on Saturday or jam in the summer. Knowing who tells the best jokes and where to go for a good drink." She gestured to the lake. "Knowing the best makeout places, and learning from years of experience so you don't damage yourself while having a good time."

As she'd hoped, that made him laugh. Cade's entire face lit up, the remnants of anger behind his eyes fading as he looked around the lake with an affectionate smile.

"Best makeout places, huh?"

"Word is, this is yours," she said, not only ready to change the subject, but desperate to see what kind of magic happened when the lovemaking was done right.

"You don't say?" he asked, shifting around to face her, his hands cupping her hips and his gaze intent on her mouth. "You know better than anyone that gossip isn't always reliable."

"Word is," she repeated in a whisper. Eyelids heavy, she stared at his mouth, reveling in the soft fullness of his lips and hint of stubble that kept his face just this side of pretty.

His fingers were gentle as he reached up to glide over her cheek, tucking her hair behind one ear, then leaning down to brush his lips over her jaw.

"Word isn't everything," he said quietly. "Gossip always skims the surface, but never touches the truth."

"Are you trying to say the gossip isn't true? That this wasn't your special place?" she asked, already knowing the answer but wanting to hear it from him. Wanting him to say something, anything, that'd make her feel like she was different than the other girls he'd brought here.

That she was more.

That she was special.

But he didn't say a word.

He just looked at her.

The expression in his eyes was intense. Like he was searching her soul. Weighing, waiting. She didn't know what he found, or what he'd do with the discovery. Was she worthy of him, of his special place?

Nerves added a painful edge to the desire coursing through Eden. Before she could figure out what to do, find anything to say to break the tension, Cade skimmed both hands into the thick strands of her hair, cupping his fingers behind her head and angling her mouth to his.

His lips flowed, like a whisper, over hers. She barely

had time for a taste before he moved on, brushing kisses
over her cheek, along her jaw and down her throat.

Her system spun into overdrive, passion smothering the
nerves as she melted under his touch. Her fingers tingled
as they skimmed over the hard muscles of his shoulders,
down his back and cupped his tight butt. His body was a
work of art. One she wanted to fully appreciate this time.
To study, to explore, to enjoy.

Cade's kisses trailed along the rounded collar of her
T-shirt, soft and sweet, as his fingers danced down her
side, down to where the hem met her jeans. His hands,
hot and powerful, slid under the fabric. She sucked in her
breath, flattening her belly as his fingers pressed higher.
They trailed the wide band of her bra, scraping the length
of her torso with his fingernails. She shivered, her breath
catching on a low moan.

Desire flamed.

Need pounded.

She grabbed the back of his shirt, tugging hard to pull
the material from the waistband of his jeans. As soon as
the shirt cleared, her fingers were scrambling for skin,
smoothing over the hard, hot flesh of his back before skimming around to tangle in the delicious sprinkling of hair
climbing from his flat belly up to a vee between his pecs.

His body was freaking awesome.

And his hands.

She moaned when he cupped his entire palm over her
now bare breast. When had he unhooked her bra? He
rubbed in circles, warming, caressing, tormenting her
nipple into a hard pebble.

She knew it wasn't a race, but she still hurried to keep
up, angling so she could scrape gentle nails over his nipples. He growled.

Before she could take another breath, he'd stripped

her shirt and bra off, tossing them somewhere toward the bushes and grabbing her by the waist to lift her high.

For a second, he just stared. His eyes were slits, passion flaming like a conflagration in the green depths as he took in the sight of her. Eden, needing more, desperate to push him over the edge, unbuttoned her jeans and gave a gentle push so they slid off her hips. They caught on her shoes, leaving her naked from the knees up except for a tiny pair of purple lace panties.

His groan was lost as his mouth latched onto her breast, his lips skating over the soft flesh to the aching tip. He sucked, hard. Her body convulsed, her core as hot and wet as he was making her nipple. There was something amazingly erotic about being so much at his mercy that she was practically floating on air.

He nipped, his teeth scraping her flesh, his mouth still sucking hard. Eden's fingers dug into his shoulders and she gave a whimpering cry of encouragement.

"More," she insisted. "Make me come."

"I'm gonna make you come more than once," he said, pulling back to stare into her eyes. The intensity of his look echoed the promise in his words.

"Big talk," she teased.

He laughed, then set her on the ground, but his hands didn't leave her waist. A thrill of delight shivered through her at the idea that he didn't want to let her go, even for a second.

"Off," he demanded, his words low.

"You first," she shot back.

He frowned, then, his fingers tightened for a second before he released her. His clothes were tossed aside so fast, Eden wasn't sure he had any buttons left, even on his jeans. She kicked off her shoes, toed off her socks and in the second it took her to step out of her jeans, he was naked.

She almost tripped over her pile of clothes at the sight.

"Oh, my," she breathed. Eyes huge, she tried to take him in. He was gorgeous.

Golden skin stretched over a body that would make a goddess weep. Sculpted muscles flowed in swimmer form, wide shoulders tapering down to a narrow waist and thighs...

Her mouth actually watered.

Oh, his thighs. Long, lean and roped with tight muscles, they were the perfect frame for the jutting length of manhood waving hello between them.

Eden's own knees got a little weak at that point.

"I guess you've got what it takes to live up to that *more than once* promise," she observed, her tone almost reverent. Unable to resist, she reached out to run her fingers along the hard, long length of him. He hissed. She angled a wicked grin his way, then did it again.

Before he could grab her and take control, she dropped to her knees. Palms flat, she ran her hands up the back of his legs from his calves to his upper thighs, then grabbed his butt for a little squeeze. At the same time, she leaned close and blew a puff of air on the rounded tip of his erection.

He growled.

She swirled her tongue around the head, lapping at the velvety knob before sucking, just that tip, into her mouth.

His fingers tunneled into her hair, the tips digging into her scalp as if he was afraid she'd pull away.

As if. She'd just been served up a huge portion of the tastiest treat she'd ever seen. She might never be done. She didn't think she could ever get enough of him.

Her lips tight against his flesh, she slid her mouth as far down as she could, then pulled back to just the tip, sucked, and did it again. And again. And again.

Cade could only take so much. Flesh quivering, he shifted, stepping backward. From her position on her knees, Eden slanted him a pouty look. And why not? He'd just taken away her treat.

He bent, grabbing his jeans and digging out his wallet before tossing them aside.

"While you're down there," he suggested, handing her a condom.

"My pleasure," Eden murmured with a wicked smile, sure it was going to be just that. Her eyes locked on his, she tore open the foil wrapper. Before she slid the latex over his burgeoning length, though, she leaned in for another kiss.

"You're wicked," he claimed, somewhere between a laugh and a moan. His fingers slid into her hair, a combination of a plea and a caress. Eden didn't know when she'd ever felt this wonderful, this powerful.

She had her hottest fantasy, panting over her.

It was amazing.

Ready to see just how much more amazing it could get, she slid the condom over his erection. Before she could move, he lifted her off her knees and in a single fluid motion laid himself back on the grass and positioned her above him.

"You're gorgeous," he told her. His eyes feasted on her body as she settled her knees on either side of his hips, his hands going to her breasts like they were magnetically drawn. His fingers tweaked the tips even as his palms held the weight, cupping and squeezing gently.

Eden's body heated, wet and needy as if every shift of his hands pushed her higher, hotter. Her hands braced on his chest for balance, she leaned over to kiss him at the same time she slowly, oh, baby, so incredibly slowly, lowered herself on the hard length of him.

He filled her.

Completed her.

Like they were custom fit, her body took him all, shivering and pulsing around him. For a second, Eden couldn't move. She could only feel. Sensation after sensation rippled from her core to her nipples and back again.

Cade groaned.

Swallowing hard, she lifted her hips. Then slowly, twisting a little, brought them back down so her core was pressed tight against the thatch of curls at his groin.

Cade growled.

Eden did it again. She moved faster. Up and down. Sliding, undulating. Her body grasping at his in desperate need. He moaned his approval, letting her set the pace.

Her eyes still on his, she watched his face tighten, his eyes hooded as they languidly moved from hers, then down to her breasts where his fingers were working pure magic, then back again. It was like he was fascinated with her body. Obsessed even.

The very idea made her come a little.

More excited than she'd ever been, Eden moved faster.

The power built, tighter, needier.

Her head fell back, her body on fire as she rode the waves of sensations crashing around her. Her pounding heart echoed the power of her orgasms, beating like a conga drum.

Hands trembling, she gripped Cade's shoulders.

His fingers tightened, holding her breasts high as he angled his body upward to lick one, then the other nipple. Back and forth his mouth went, making her crazy as the climax coiled, tight as a spring, in her belly.

Then he nipped, his teeth tugging one nipple into his mouth to be sucked, laved, teased. His fingers twisted the other, then he tugged.

Eden exploded. Her moans were whimpers now as she

rode the waves, ebbing and flowing with pleasure. He followed her with a guttural growl of delight, his body pulsing inside hers.

It was like floating on a cloud of passion. Spikes of pleasure shot like lightening through her, but didn't change the foggy haze of delight that she was riding.

"More," she whispered, leaning down to press a soft kiss against his chin, then scattering more along his jaw and cheeks. "You're yummy, and I'm hungry."

"Feast, baby," he encouraged, his tone just as satisfied as the look on his gorgeous face.

11

EDEN GRADUALLY DRIFTED AWAKE on the bank of the lake. Was this what an out-of-body experience felt like? Gloriously delicious, as if everything had a surreal tint to it. From her body, which ached in the most deliciously satisfied way, to her senses. She slowly lifted her eyelids to peer into the evening light. The sun was setting, the lake bathed in a rainbow of pinks, oranges and purples to reflect the evening sky. Cade's body was wrapped around hers, protective and warm.

She blinked a couple of times, not sure what'd woken her. She was limp with sexual satisfaction. So why the sudden tension? Like she should be worried, or even scared.

Then he muttered in his sleep, his hands gripping her waist as if he'd just been shoved off a cliff and she was his only hope of not plummeting to the ground.

Eden came fully awake, but was still standing on the edge of a terrifying nightmare. She couldn't see it, but she knew it was there. And it was attacking Cade. She could feel the waves of misery pouring off him.

"No!" His denial was guttural, desperate, even though it was only a whisper.

Frowning, she tried to shift. But his fingers dug in

tighter. She tilted her head back, peering up at him. Fear melted into sympathy. Her heart ached at the desolation on his face, at the pain in his voice.

"Cade," she whispered. She reached up to his shoulder, giving him a gentle shake. "Wake up."

"No. Return fire. Stop. No!" He didn't yell. He barely muttered the words. But the intensity, the horror in them ripped at Eden's gut, terrifying her.

"Cade. Wake up," she demanded, shaking harder now. "What?"

For one second, she could see it all in his eyes. The miserable pain, the devastation. The soul-wrenching loss.

Then he blinked. All it took was a second for him to tuck it all away. Charm and a rueful sort of self-derision replaced the raw emotion on his face.

"I think we wore each other out," he said, his smile a shadow of its usual wattage, his laugh a little rough around the edges. "I can't believe we fell asleep."

"You were dreaming," she said, ignoring the hint to let it go. "Are you okay?"

His jaw clenched, then he shifted, so he could skim his bottom hand down to cup her bare butt and his upper hand toward her breast.

Before he could cup her already aching flesh, she grabbed his wrist.

"You were dreaming," she said again. At least, if being under emotional attack in one's sleep counted as dreaming. Eden's eyes flew over his face, trying to see if he was okay. Stress etched lines in the corners of his eyes, bracketed his mouth. But his lips were curved in his usual, charming smile and his beautiful green gaze was determined. To fight the demons? Or to push her away?

"That's what people do when they are asleep." Whether because he saw how determined she was, or out of pique that she wasn't ready to roll around on the bank again, Cade shifted. He pulled his arms away and sat upright. "It's going to get cold, though. We should head back."

Eden gave him a long, considering look.

Here she was at the lake, that magical place of sexual-fantasies-come-true. With the sexiest man in the world. One who'd just rocked her every idea of what pleasure was supposed to feel like. If she ever wanted to feel that rocking pleasure again, she was pretty sure she should let it go. Just let the subject change, gather up her underwear and drag him back to her bed for another round.

But she couldn't.

This was Cade.

Her hero.

The guy who was always there for her. To save her from falling out of trees. To shoo away the mean girls. To show her that her fantasies had nothing on reality.

Didn't she owe it to him to be there for him, too?

Even if it ruined her shot at another mind-blowing orgasm?

Feeling very self-sacrificing, and just a little worried, she ignored the tense ball of stress in her stomach and rubbed her hand over his bare shoulder.

"Cade," she prompted softly, her tone as sweet as it was stubborn. "What's wrong? Were you dreaming about your friend? The one you lost last year?"

Maybe she should have got up and kneed him in the balls. He'd probably have looked less betrayed.

"Gossip again?" he asked in a tone as chilly as one of his father's worst put-downs. "I thought you knew better than to believe the whispers on the street."

"You told me yourself that you lost your friend, Phil," Eden countered, irritated at being lumped into the same category as the gossips, but deciding to letting it go. If she was hurting, she'd lash out, too. "I know how close you were because your grandmother speaks of him often. Last year she showed me a huge stack of pictures of the two of you and your other friend. Blake, right? She's referred to you three as *those sweet boys* ever since you brought them home for Christmas a few years ago."

For just a second, he closed his eyes as if the memory was too painful to see. Then he looked at her, his eyes as cold as she'd ever seen.

Eden swallowed hard, suddenly very aware that she was naked.

"Grandmother shouldn't be talking about my friends. Or about me. I didn't realize she was as much of a gossip as the rest of the town," he groused, shoving his hand through his hair and glaring across the water.

"She needed help putting photos into the family album," Eden said, irritation banishing her self-consciousness. How dare he so easily assume they were gossiping. "Your father has no interest, you weren't home and she doesn't like to let just anyone poke through her pictures. I'd stopped by to bring her a pie and offered to do it for her. She didn't gossip. She simply told me the names to write next to each entry."

"Oh."

He sounded like he'd rather have had that kick to the balls.

As he should.

"Yes, oh," Eden snapped back, sitting up and grabbing his shirt to wrap around her, definitely uncomfortable with her nudity now. His was fine, though. Even irritated, she could appreciate perfection when it sat naked in front of her. "Maybe instead of jumping to rude conclusions, you should consider how much Catherine worries about you. How much she loves you."

His shrug was a guilty jerk of one shoulder.

Eden pulled her knees up to her chest and took a deep breath. She felt like crying. Both for Cade's misery, and at the realization that she'd been so, so shallow.

All she'd ever seen was the gorgeous guy next door. The hottie who pulled her out of scrapes, who kept her supplied in fantasy material. That he was a navy SEAL only added to his sexy persona.

Sure, a few days ago on the cliffs, she'd clued in that his job had risks. That there was more to being a hero than just riding in with a charming smile and great timing. But she'd sort of let that fade into the back of her head. Not because it didn't matter, she realized, wrapping her arms tighter around her knees. But because it was scary to think of what he must face on a regular basis. To admit, even just to herself, to the possibility of something happening to him.

"I'm sorry you had a—" What? Bad dream sounded so childish. Nightmare was too B movie-esque. "Troubled sleep. I wish the sex had been a little wilder. Maybe then you'd have been too exhausted to dream."

She offered a tremulous smile, giving him her best *aren't I cute* look.

For a second, he just looked stunned. Then he burst into laughter.

"Oh, I don't know. I thought it was pretty wild," he said, reaching back to give her a quick, one-armed hug. He didn't keep up contact, though. Just as soon as his arm fell away, so did his smile.

Eden's heart ached.

As always, unable to sit quietly in the face of suffering, she rubbed a comforting hand on his shoulder again.

"I'm so sorry," she murmured. "And not sorry, in a hey, open a wound and share it with me kind of way. I just hate to see you hurting like this. And hiding from the hurt."

She wanted to tell him that it didn't do any good to hide like that. That he should get it out, whatever it was. Air the pain so it could start healing.

But she couldn't. She knew whatever she was imagining, whatever she'd lived through, couldn't compare to his pain. Who was she to tell someone how to grieve?

All she could do was be there for him, ache for him.

After a handful of miserably long minutes, Cade shrugged again.

"It was my mission," he finally said, his focus so strong on the water, it was like he was confessing a sin to the lake gods. "I planned it, I led it."

"Was it your first?"

"Nah." He shook his head. "I've led dozens. Not just like this, no two are exactly the same. But similar. Same region, same objective."

"Something went wrong?" she asked quietly.

"Phil was hit. Shrapnel to the head. One minute he was cracking jokes, the next he was gone. He still had a smile on his face when he hit the ground."

Tears trickled off Eden's chin, horror filling her heart as she imagined how he must have felt to have that happen right before his eyes.

"It wasn't your fault," she protested, shifting across the grass until she sat next to him. She shoved aside the sudden cascading barrage of terror that'd come along with recognizing the reality of his job and tried to focus on helping Cade. He still didn't look her way. Just continued to stare at the water, his face as hard as marble.

"The mission was my responsibility."

Eden didn't know what to say to that. She understood responsibility. Knew the heavy weight of it and how tempting it was to shoulder it alone. But she also recognized guilt. Why did the two always seem to go hand in hand?

She should let it go. She should make a joke, change the subject, slide down his body and offer a blowjob as a distraction.

Anything to keep him from thinking about his friend.

But she couldn't. Not when he was so clearly hurting.

"Could you have stopped it from happening?" she asked quietly. "Could you have done anything to change it?"

He still didn't look at her. Just stared at the water. His lips were white in the moonlight, his shoulders rigid. Finally, after long, miserably drawn-out seconds, he shrugged. "The powers that be don't think so."

"Do you?" She bit her lip, knowing she'd be better off backing away. But she'd never been able to take the safe route. "Does your friend Blake?"

That got his attention.

Cade's gaze shot to hers like a sniper's bullet. Iced fury flamed in those green depths, made all the scarier because the rest of his features were now shrouded in the dark.

The charming facade that most people took as the regular Cade Sullivan cracked, showing the real man beneath the usual charismatic amiability. Eden almost took a step back.

"I'm just saying…" She almost stuttered, then took a deep breath and continued, "Maybe you shouldn't be blaming yourself. I've seen all those pictures of you and Phil and Blake. You look like really good friends. Would Phil blame you? Would he want you carrying this?"

"Phil isn't here anymore," Cade snapped. "So what he would or wouldn't have wanted is immaterial."

Eden's heart broke for him. The pain, the loss, the misery. Without that protective facade of charm he usually held between himself and everyone else, she could see them all so clearly on his face.

She'd only been interested in the fantasy. In hot, wild

sex and a chance to live out all those things she'd dreamed of for so many years with a man she had always hero worshipped. Now he was more than a hero. Cade was a man, all man.

A man that she was terrified to realize she could easily fall in love with.

CADE WANTED TO TELL HER this was hardly the love talk he usually enjoyed after incredible sex. He liked the manly feel of cuddling in the afterglow. He preferred a slow buildup to round two, maybe a little kissing and sucking.

A woman poking at his most vulnerable parts, and not the one between his legs, wasn't the makings of a turn-on.

"You're a hero, Cade. Not because of your job, or because you've earned a chestful of medals. But because of who you are inside. Because you care, deeply, about people and about doing what's right." Eden bit her lip, then sighed and gestured to the patch of grass across the lake. "You take responsibility for everyone. For everything. Even when it's not yours to take."

Cade sighed. She wasn't going to give it up, was she.

"I was in charge," he said, appreciating her attempts to make him feel better but not willing to sidestep reality. "That means the responsibility was all mine."

Eden nodded.

Then, as if she'd heard his mental instructions, she shifted closer to his body, smoothed the palm of her hand up, then down his chest. The vulnerable part he wanted her interested in stirred to life as she pressed a soft kiss to a scar zigzagging down his shoulder.

"That must be rough. Taking all those untrained, unskilled, and what? Unwilling guys into a battle."

Shocked fury shut down his libido in a flash.

"What?" He ripped his gaze from the safe view of the

trees to glare at her. "That's bullshit. My team is the best. They are SEALs, dammit. We never ran a mission unless they were totally on board, were totally ready to kick ass. There's nobody unwilling to serve in my squad."

Eden didn't say a word. She waited a beat, then arched one brow.

Cade's frown turned ferocious.

"I'm not saying Phil didn't know what he was doing, or that he wasn't damned good," he snapped, getting the message loud and clear. "But—"

"Either your guys are damned good, highly trained and totally prepared, and the loss of one of them was a horrible result of going into battle," she interrupted. "Or you were responsible for every single thing, from the weather to the enemy to the state of mind of every man under your command."

Unable to find a valid argument that'd shoot her down, Cade finally settled on a glare.

She gave him a sympathetic smile, cupping his cheek in her palm and pressing a kiss against his lips.

Then she shifted, rolling quickly so her body angled over his. Straddling him, her thighs gripped his hips and her glorious breasts pressed against his chest.

"What are you doing?" he gasped as his body sprang to full alert.

"Exhausting you," she said with a watery laugh. Thankfully, her face was dry now, clear of those tears that ripped at his gut. "I don't know of any other way to distract you from making yourself miserable."

Cade wanted to protest. To claim that he wasn't miserable. But she wasn't leaving him any room to argue.

Or much space for self-pity.

Because it was impossible to feel bad when her body was making his feel so good.

Damn, Cade groaned as she snagged another of the condoms and rolled it over his throbbing length. Then she slid back up, her thighs gripping his sides as she slowly— so, so slowly—impaled herself on his rock-hard erection.

She was delicious.

Glorious. Like a triumphant Valkyrie warrior, fighting his demons for him, then sweeping him away to the heavens.

He was usually the one who rode to the rescue. Who dove in and saved the day.

Just before he took her mouth again, he had to wonder...

Who was going to rescue him?

CADE CROSSED HIS HANDS behind his head and propped one bare foot on the other, waiting for Eden to join him in bed.

This was pretty damned awesome. He'd never done this domestic thing with a woman before. A night here or there, a few days at a plush resort once in a while, sure. But all week long, everything from meals to sleep to showers? This was a whole new world. One he'd have sworn he'd hate. Instead, he was loving it.

He suddenly understood what Blake was talking about. That feeling of completion. Of happiness. It was freaky. Hell, another few days and he'd be writing bad poetry and crying over afternoon specials. A week and he'd be thinking about baby names and retirement property.

Cade grimaced, feeling like a girl all of a sudden.

Maybe he should drop to the floor and do a hundred pushups. Go flex something in the mirror.

His cell phone buzzed. Grateful for the distraction, he reached over to check the incoming text.

Did you get my money?

Or maybe he'd go beat the hell out of something to relieve frustration, he added to the previous litany.

Damn, his father was a pain.

Cade's fingers hovered over the text keyboard. He wanted to write back that the loan wasn't Eden's to pay. That Robert was an idiot for lending Eleanor money so it was his problem to collect. That Cade wasn't his damned errand boy.

But he didn't type any of that.

Because none of it would make a damned bit of difference. The minute he tossed this back in Robert's face, the old man would come after Eden directly.

She was doing great. Getting her business going, paying off the bank loan her mother had dumped on her. She didn't need this, too. It was Eleanor's responsibility, just like the bank loan. Cade wasn't going to let Eden get railroaded into paying Robert. After trying for a week and a half to reach the elder Gillespie, he'd finally had to accept that it wasn't going to happen before he went back to Coronado.

So…on to Plan B.

Cade glanced at the bathroom door. He couldn't hear the shower anymore. She'd be out any second now. So he took a deep breath, made one of those split-second decisions that made him an effective SEAL and texted back:

You'll have a check tomorrow.

Cade tossed the phone on the nightstand.

So the check would have his name on the signatory line, not Eden or Eleanor's. Robert could just deal with it. Then, when Cade finally heard from Eleanor, he'd make arrangements for her to pay him instead.

There, he gave a mental clap of his hands. All taken care of.

Except maybe he should tell Eden about it.

But what good would that do? It'd just stress her out, add to her worries and mess up his last days with her.

He closed his eyes, taking a deep breath and shoring up his determination.

He'd tell her later. After sex.

And after he told her he was heading back to San Diego in four days.

Never, since the day he left for boot camp, had Cade wanted less to return to duty. And not just because of the gorgeous woman joining him in bed.

Although she was a big part of the reason.

But so were the nightmares. The intense, gut-wrenching pain of missing Phil. The doubts about his leadership, the second-guessing of his decisions. Cade wasn't sure he had what it took to do a good job anymore. He wasn't sure he could be a SEAL.

For a man whose confidence had always topped out at supreme, this wasn't just humiliating, it was confusing as hell. He didn't know what to do.

So he wasn't going to do anything. For now, his entire focus was Eden. On fixing her issues, making her life easier. His, he'd deal with later.

"WELL?" FEELING FRESH and sexy after her shower, Eden sat cross-legged on her bed and leaned over to peer into Cade's face. "Aren't you going to say anything?"

He peeled one eye open and gave her a languid look. It took all her control not to giggle, but she managed to keep her expression impatiently expectant.

"I could say I'm looking forward to some good lovin'. Or I could say good-night, since it's almost midnight and you had me up early this morning to take care of a goat." He sounded a lot happier about the former than the latter.

Probably because Jojo hadn't taken too kindly to a man in her pen and had tried to headbutt him right back out.

"It won't be good lovin'. It will be great," Eden corrected primly. Then she arched one brow. "And you had a nap while I saw clients this afternoon, so I'd think you caught up on sleep just fine."

Eden wasn't quite sure what to make of her new life. She just knew it was wonderful. Somehow, in the week since the lakeside lovemaking, Cade had sort of moved in with her. Sort of, because neither of them had actually said a word about it. But his clothes were in a drawer she'd cleared. His toiletries sat next to hers in the bathroom. And the last three nights, she'd come in from a packed day at the clinic to find dinner waiting on the table, Cade in his stocking feet reading the paper and looking about as content as she'd ever seen him.

Business was booming, her love life was rocking and her social life… Holy cow, her social life. Suddenly she was the most popular girl in town. She'd been invited to join committees, to luncheons and just yesterday, Crystal had called to chat and ask about adopting the kittens.

It was like she suddenly belonged.

All thanks to Cade.

"Okay," her naked hero said, opening both eyes now and giving her a questioning look. Beneath the query and sexual heat, though, she could see something else. A pain that wrenched at her heart. A pain she didn't know how to fix. How to heal. All she could do was the same thing she'd done all week. Distract him with sex. But as deliciously wonderful as the results of that were, she knew that sooner or later, he had to face the pain. She just didn't know how to help him.

"What were you asking about?" At her blank look, he

arched a brow and added, "You asked if I had anything to say, remember?"

"Remember? Oh, yeah," she said with a strained laugh. "You visited with your grandmother today, right? How is she doing with Alfie?"

The look on Cade's face was pure doubt. "Are you sure that's a dog? It sounds more like one of the squeaky toys you find at the pet store. It's about the same size, too."

"Alfie's an AKC-registered Yorkshire Terrier," Eden said with an offended sniff. Then she grinned. "Isn't he adorable? As soon as you told me that your grandmother wanted a companion dog, I knew he'd be perfect. The lady who'd been taking care of him almost refused to give him up, but she already has ten dogs of her own."

Cade's jaw dropped. "Ten? Granted, they're so small, it would take about ten of them to equal the size of a real dog. But...ten?"

"She's a breeder who takes in fosters from time to time," Eden chided gently. "We're lucky she had the perfect pet so quickly. Sometimes it can take months. But I think it was love at first sight for both Alfie and Catherine."

"Yeah, she's totally into the dog," he admitted. "She was personally making it oatmeal and steamed carrots when I stopped by this afternoon."

"That's great. Alfie's fourteen and used to a whole-food diet." Eden gave him a narrow-eyed look. "What's the matter? Are you jealous of your grandmother's new pet?"

"She has a cook, but she insists on doing it herself. I don't think she's made me lunch since I was two," he muttered, making Eden grin.

"You are jealous," she said with a laugh.

"Only of the time you spend away from me," he admitted, his hand skimming up her thigh and underneath her nightgown.

Eden's breath caught. Desire shimmered, low in her belly.

"I'm with you now," she said.

"So you are." In a swift move, he rolled over, taking her with him. Laughing, Eden cuddled into the pillow and looked up at his sexy face.

"Let's go away this weekend," he suggested, burying his face in her throat for a nuzzle. "Just us. We'll go anywhere you want. Dancing all night in the city. A romantic balloon ride in wine country. You name it."

"I can't. We can't," she corrected. "This weekend is the Spring Fling, remember?"

"We'll skip it."

"Your grandmother would kill us both."

Cade's groan reverberated against her throat, but he didn't argue further. If anything, he got serious about turning the heat up on his kisses.

Eden shivered in delight, her hands cruising over the hard breadth of his shoulders.

As much as she wanted that feeling of being a couple, taking a trip together, she wanted the memory of walking into the most prestigious event of the year on the arm of Cade Sullivan. The most popular guy in Ocean Point.

That memory would be the cherry on top of a deliciously sexy, mind-bogglingly amazing fantasy come true. Walking in with Cade would cement her place in society.

The joy faded a little, happiness taking on a dim edge. Her heart drooped like a flower in desperate need of water as she forced herself to finish that thought.

She'd have wonderful memories. She'd be a part of the clique that she'd been born into, but only skirted around the edges of for most of her life. She'd have enough clients to pay off her mother's loan, a solid business and a strong foundation to build her future on.

The only thing she wouldn't have was Cade.

12

THE SPRING FLING. Ocean Point's most prestigious social event of the year, and here she was. Not helping the bartender, or sitting at the hostess table by the entrance, checking off RSVPs.

Nope. Eden was dressed in her fanciest gown, wearing her sassiest shoes, dancing in the arms of the sexiest man in town.

She gave a little shiver of delight. Wow, so many wonderful things were happening in her life, it was as if the dreams-come-true fairy had dumped a whole bagful of wishes on her life.

It felt magnificent.

Almost as magnificent as dancing in Cade's arms. Except instead of looking like he was having the time of his life, Cade was tenser than she'd ever seen him. Oh, the usual charm was right there, front and center. And he was just as gorgeous today as he'd been two weeks ago, or even a year ago. That hadn't changed. But Eden was pretty sure this was the first time she'd ever seen him so ill-at-ease. She rubbed a soothing hand over his back, grateful to feel some of the tension drain as he gave her a little smile.

Torn between the delight of the moment and needing

to make Cade feel better, Eden hesitated for just a second. Then, unable to do otherwise, she leaned in to brush a kiss on his cheek.

"Catherine and the Spring Fling committee did a wonderful job with everything. But maybe we could cut out early. Go home, get naked, heat up some cherry-flavored body oil," she added with a teasing wink.

She'd learned to read him pretty well over the last week or so. To look beyond his eyes, which hid everything behind a layer of charm, and instead notice the tiny wrinkles that pinched the corners of his eyes when he was stressed.

And despite her offer of warm body oil and a quick escape, the wrinkles were still there.

But all Cade said was, "Now that's an idea. But I promised my grandmother I'd introduce the Veteran's Auction."

"Then we'll leave as soon as it's over?"

"The very second."

Figuring she'd better enjoy the few dances she'd get, Eden cuddled closer into his arms with a sigh and glanced around. It was a magical scene. The chandeliers and candles all glinted warmly. The scent of lilies filled the air, melding with subtle perfumes and rich cologne. Like Cinderella at the ball, Eden reveled in the sight of everyone dressed so beautifully, looking so fancy.

Well, hell. A lot of those beautifully dressed people weren't just looking fancy. They were staring. Hard.

"So this is what it's like to be royalty," she murmured, giving Cade a flutter of her lashes as she burrowed a little deeper into his arms as the string quartet's rendition of The Doors's "Light My Fire" played. "I feel like I should be doing the princess wave."

From a few of the looks shooting her way, the wave would be returned with a single-finger salute. Of course, those were all single women who had crushes on Cade, so she shouldn't be surprised.

"I'd rather you kept your hands on me instead of waving to the gawkers," he said, taking his attention away from her face for just a second to cast a derisive look to the staring crowd. Not that they were the only ones on the dance floor. But they were the only ones cell phone cameras were being aimed at. "Just ignore them. We're here to dance, to help my grandmother raise a bundle of money, then to get the hell out and have fun."

With a tiny shiver in honor of the last round of fun they'd had, Eden smiled her agreement. Dance, help, money, run. She was good with all of that. And maybe if she focused on those steps, she could ignore the stares. Was this what he had to deal with all the time? The paparazzi-like frenzy from his friends and hometown acquaintances? She hadn't realized how bad it was for him, always being the center of attention.

A flash of color caught her eye, the vividness of Janie's dress commanding Eden's, and quite a few other people's, attention. The green tulle was just a few shades brighter than the jealous heat in her eyes as she glared.

Eden shifted, missing a step and almost stomping on Cade's foot. Before she could even wince, he easily incorporated her stumble into their dance steps.

"What's wrong?" he asked.

"Just feeling a little self-conscious," she answered, pulling her gaze away from the crowd. For a second she stared at his shoulder, before lifting her eyes to meet his. "I think I'd be more comfortable dancing without the audience."

"Could we be naked?"

She blinked, then burst into laughter. Her fingers curled tighter around the back of his neck and she gave him a flirtatious look.

"We could. Or better yet, we could take a radio down to the lake and dance there. Naked *and* under the moonlight."

They grinned at each other for a second. Then, remembering how many times they'd made love by the lake, and in her bedroom, her kitchen, her office, her bathroom, heck, everywhere but her car because it was still in the body shop, they stopped.

"Why don't we go outside and practice?" he whispered huskily, his breath warming her ear before he brushed a soft kiss against her cheek.

"A walk outside would be nice," she finally agreed, giving him a shadow of a smile. It would give her a few seconds to regroup, maybe a kiss or two to remind herself of why being with Cade was a wonderful temporary fantasy that she should enjoy every second of, and then, she'd be just fine.

Warm and comforting, his hand curled around hers as he led her off the dance floor. They'd made it about halfway to the wide expanse of French doors when Cade's steps slowed. She looked up at him.

His smile had dimmed and tension deepened the wrinkles in the sides of his eyes, stiffened his shoulders. Eden followed his gaze, grimacing when she saw his father settled into the corner with his glass of scotch, unlit cigar and group of toadies.

"I guess I should pay my respects," Cade said in the same tone she figured he'd use to accept an order to throw himself on a live grenade.

Eden's smile didn't waver, but she did take a deep, fortifying breath before entwining her fingers tighter with his and nodding. "Sure, let's say hello."

"You're going with me?"

"You sound so shocked."

"I am. Why would you want to talk to him? I sure

wouldn't if I had a choice." He slanted her an odd look, like he was about to change his mind about greeting his father.

"Moral support," she said, nudging him with her shoulder and pulling him another step forward. "C'mon. Let's get it over with so we can make out in the garden."

That got both a smile, and more importantly, his feet moving. They didn't make it two yards before their path was intersected by another man dressed in navy whites.

"Uncle Seth," Cade said in shock. "What are you doing here?"

"Can't a guy drop in to visit his favorite nephew?"

"I'm your only nephew."

"Then let's call it a friendly visit," the older man said before giving Cade an arch look and nodding to Eden.

Cade shook his head, as if clearing a ringing from his ears, then lifted Eden's hand in his. "Uncle Seth, this is Eden Gillespie. Eden, my uncle, Captain Seth Borden."

"Captain?" Eden offered a smile and a warm handshake. "Do you serve with Cade?"

"We're on the same base. But I'm in training. Something Cade here will be great at. I'm hoping he'll take me up on the offer to come work with the BUDS."

"You moonlighting as a recruiter now?" Cade asked. His smile was friendly, but his tone had a sharp edge to it.

Tension spiked, sharp and dangerous. Unlike the two men, Eden was unused to battles, so she felt like it was going to smother her. She shifted from one foot to the other, trying to find something to say to defuse the situation.

What had the other man said? Why was his offer— whatever it was—such an issue?

"Nah, just a guy with an intense interest in your future." Seth's smile shifted, worry lighting his eyes as he gave his nephew a long look. "A guy's got to know when he's approaching burnout. When it's time to take a break and look at some options."

What was he talking about?

Cade was approaching burnout? She gave a tiny grimace, noting that he looked more like he was battling fury rather than exhaustion.

"Eden, will you excuse us?" Cade asked, not taking his eyes off his uncle.

"Sure," she said, her own gaze huge as it sprang from one man's tense face to the other. "I'll mingle. It was a pleasure to meet you."

Other than Seth's absent nod, neither of them acknowledged her. Instead, after Cade gestured toward the open patio doors, they both strode out like they were going to strip down and beat the crap out of each other.

Eden's heart raced, nerves jangling.

Cade was a big boy.

He'd cut his teeth on society events, and this one was sponsored by his grandmother. He wouldn't do anything to cause a scene.

And he definitely wouldn't appreciate any interference on Eden's part.

Now that she had all of those reasonable, well-thought-out details solid in her mind, Eden gave a satisfied sigh.

Then looked around for Cade's grandmother.

She was going to need some backup when she went out to interrupt that little talk.

There.

She saw Catherine across the room, holding court in a Valentino gown and a diamond necklace and holding a tiny dog in her arm.

Aww, Alfie was here? Even if she didn't want, desperately, to congratulate the elderly woman on breaking rules with such panache, Eden would have rushed over just to see the dog.

She was almost there when someone called her name. Frowning, she glanced over to see Robert, his usual glower in place, beckoning.

"You bellowed?" she asked with a friendly smile as she approached his table. He sat in the corner, away from the dance floor, where it was quieter. With just the flick of his fingers, he sent his buddies away and gestured to the now vacated seat for Eden to join him.

"I can bellow if I want. I just had surgery," he said, chewing his unlit cigar.

Eden slid into the seat opposite him and gave his hand a sympathetic pat. "You've always bellowed, though. But you did, indeed, just have surgery. So why aren't you in bed resting?"

She couldn't help it. She knew Robert was a curmudgeonly old grump, a vicious businessman and a complete social snob. But she sort of liked him. Probably because his eyes were that same piercing green as Cade's.

"I've got business to take care of," Robert said, giving her a gruff look under his brows. As if she'd done something wrong. Eden frowned, wondering what it might be, other than having a brick wall inconveniently placed in the path of his car.

"Business? At the biggest social event of the season?" Eden noted his glass was empty and gestured to one of the waiters, then gave a tiny shake of her head when he headed for the bar. *Water,* she mouthed.

"More business is done at social events than in an office," he said, leaning forward and folding both hands together, as if preparing to prove his point.

Clueless about what kind of business he could want to talk to her about, Eden lifted her brow.

"So what's Seth doing here? Is he going to help the boy out? Did he give any indication about what he wanted to talk to Cade about?"

Was this fatherly concern? Worry over his son's recent loss? Nerves did a little dance up her spine. She wanted to help Cade, but Eden didn't think talking to his father about personal issues—any issues, actually—was a good idea.

"I'm not sure why Cade's uncle is here, or what they are discussing," she finally said.

"And you wouldn't tell me if you knew."

Eden's lips twitched but she didn't say anything. Just gave a slow shake of her head.

"You and my son, you're a thing now, right?"

Nerves were chased away by joy. She and Cade were a thing. The town thought so. The mean girls thought so, if Janie's glare on the dance floor was anything to go by. Now, even Cade's father thought so.

That meant something, right? Even though Cade was probably leaving in the next couple of weeks, this meant there might be some kind of future for them. Maybe?

The nerves were back, this time beating around inside her belly like giant bats. She'd only counted on the fantasy. The intense excitement. She hadn't let herself think about—hope for—anything after Cade left.

"It's bad enough he ran off to play hero all these years, but now he's going to give it up? For what? To be a glorified teacher?" Robert glared at the garden. Then he shifted his steely gaze back to Eden. "If he's going to drop out of the SEALs, he might as well come home and take his place at Sullivan Enterprises. You talk to him. Convince him to come back."

Drop out of being a SEAL? Shock ricocheted through Eden. Cade was leaving the SEALs? But, that's what he was. Who he was. How could he leave? Was that what his uncle was talking about? A million questions flew around her head, all of them moving too fast for her to focus on.

"Cade isn't going to change his career for me," was all she finally came up with.

"The boy just wrote a check for ten grand for you, girlie. He'll listen. But you'd better talk to him quick. He's heading back to San Diego in a couple of days. If you let him get back to that base, all bets are off."

Changing jobs?

Heading back?

Cade was leaving?

Eden's head buzzed, tears filling her eyes.

Why hadn't he told her?

She opened her mouth to ask when Cade was going. The closed it again.

What the hell did Robert mean by ten grand?

"I don't understand." Baffled, Eden shook her head again. But before she could ask what he meant, the waiter exchanged Robert's empty glass with a full one.

Without looking at it, the older man tossed back his drink. All of a sudden, his face turned red, his eyes bulged and he started coughing like crazy. He glared at the glass, then at the waiter. The man, looking terrified, pointed at Eden.

"Are you okay?" she asked, hurrying around the table. Before she got halfway, Robert's personal physician cut her off.

"It was just water," she protested, horrified that she might have sent Cade's father into a relapse.

Dr. Shaw shook his head and gave her a reassuring look.

"He should have been drinking water all along. It was just the shock of putting something healthy in his system. Don't worry, he'll be fine," he said. "He just needs to rest for a bit. C'mon, Sullivan. Let's visit the clubroom. You need some downtime."

Eden watched them totter away, her head spinning as a feeling of loss and pain wrapped around her like a tight shroud. The glow of her magical evening gone, she wanted to leave. To go home and cuddle with her animals until she came to grips with the pain that Cade was leaving.

Pressing one hand against the nausea churning in her belly, Eden tried to process the fact that the impression everyone had of the two of them being something special was a total lie. Clearly, Cade didn't think what they had was important. If he did, he'd have told her that goodbye was looming.

Not sure if she should go find Cade, or dive face-first into the chocolate fountain, Eden slowly made her way toward the garden.

She didn't make it halfway across the room before she was surrounded by a giggling gaggle of women. Even though she wanted nothing more than to talk to Cade, she knew that wasn't how the game was played here at the country club. So she forced herself to smile at the five faces circling her and greeted each by name.

"What happened to your date?" Janie asked, her tone mirroring the green of her eye-watering dress. "Cade got bored already?"

"Don't be silly. There was nothing boring about that dance. Whew, girl, you and Cade were heating up the dance floor," Crystal said, her tone teasing. Eden had to smile. Ever since the blonde had adopted those kittens, she'd been super friendly.

"Right. Not boring at all," Janie repeated with a subtle eye roll for the other women. When only one of them giggled, she quickly added, "So where is your hot date?"

"Cade's visiting with his uncle." Eden cast a quick

glance at the patio, but couldn't see anything. Were they talking about the job? Was he really thinking about leaving the SEALs? Eden had a million questions. Which made standing here all the more frustrating.

"So the rumors are true?" Janie asked, crossing her arms over her chest and giving Eden a narrow look.

What rumors? Who had time for rumors and gossip and games at a time like this? Eden was about to brush Janie off, to push through the crowd so she could continue her search for Cade. Then one of the women shouldered in front of Janie and held out her hand.

"Hi, I'm Mia. I don't think we've met. Crystal and I are cousins."

"Um, hi." Eden gave her a quick smile, but before she could offer her excuses, the woman continued.

"I know this is a lousy place to talk business, but I was hoping you had a second?"

"I hear more business is done at these social events than in an office," Eden murmured, forcing her feet to stay still. But she didn't care about the business of rumors, or the latest gossip about her and Cade. She cared about reality. And finding out just exactly what that reality would be.

"Oh, I won't go into a big spiel," Mia said with a laugh, tucking a long strand of jet black hair behind her ear. "I just wanted to make an appointment to come into your clinic."

Eden's feet stopped twitching. "The clinic? Sure, did you want to bring in your pet? I don't have my book with me but you could call tomorrow morning and I'll let you know what openings I have for Monday."

"You take calls on Sunday?" Mia exchanged a look with Crystal, who shot back a triumphant look. "Actually, I have a proposition for you. I'm a veterinarian, too. I operate a mobile unit out of Fort Bragg and would love to expand my territory. I wanted to discuss the possibility of us working together."

Wow, Robert really knew what he was talking about. Eden blinked a couple of times, trying to process the proposal. A partner? A mobile clinic? Thoughts chased ideas in an excited circle through her brain. She was going to need a little time and space to sort through them all. Ready to offer a gracious social sidestep, she gave Mia a warm smile.

"Why?" She winced. Apparently her mouth hadn't got with the program yet. Clearly, there was a reason she didn't do these social things very often. "What I mean is, I have a lot of questions. Why don't we meet tomorrow morning? My clinic, around eight?"

Mia's eyes danced as she nodded. "That's perfect. And you can thank Crystal for the why. She's been raving about her kittens for a week now. I've heard good things about your work before, of course, but there's nothing like a personal recommendation."

"A personal recommendation?" Eden gave Crystal a grateful smile. "Thank you."

Before Crystal could respond, Janie rolled her eyes and elbowed her way in front of Mia.

"Fine, fine. Pets will get care and all that great stuff." She gave both women her patented fake smile, then arched a look at Eden. "What's really important now, though, are the rumors about you and Cade Sullivan. Everyone's talking about how the two of you are a thing. But I figure that's probably as likely as The Rolling Stones showing up here to play tonight."

Eden had known she'd face curiosity.

She'd known there would be questions. Innuendo. Speculation, gossip, prying.

What she hadn't expected was hatred.

But that's what was gleaming from the pretty brunette's eyes.

"Rumors about Cade and me, hmm?" Eden said slowly, casting a quick glance around the group. Crystal looked uncomfortable, like she'd be happy to follow a topic change and Mia walked away with a show of checking her cellphone. The other surrounding women, however, looked like bulldogs. But Eden wasn't about to throw them a bone.

"Well, there are the rumors about us running off to Tahiti together to live in a grass hut and drink umbrella drinks from coconuts. Mrs. Carmichael told me that one. Then there's the one about Cade using my veterinary clinic as a base for a secret SEAL operation. Did you hear about that? I wonder if he's going to let Jojo the goat help out?"

A few lips twitched. But Janie just glared.

Eden's stomach clenched.

Nerves danced, making her ears buzz a little with stage fright.

This was it. Her chance to cement her spot in the popular hall of fame. To claim Cade-ette status and revel in adulation for the rest of her single days. This would wipe out talk of Kenny's broken foot and at least three other clumsy debacles people brought up when they talked about her.

She opened her mouth to stake her claim, but no words came out.

"Oh, please," Janie dismissed, dropping the society facade altogether in her irritation. "I knew there wasn't any truth to the rumors. This whole dating thing is just another one of Cade Sullivan's rescue missions. If you had anything real going on, you'd have applied to join the Cade-ettes."

"Is that like applying for a job? Is there an interview? Do you think they need my social security number?" Eden asked, suddenly pissed.

And not, as she should rightfully be, at Janie. But at herself. What the hell had she been thinking? She suddenly felt like a total idiot. First, for letting herself fall so hard for Cade. Second, for caring so much what these women thought that she'd let herself get into this situation, with her heart at risk.

She couldn't do it.

The words, ones she'd been wanting to say for years, stuck in her throat. She bit her lip, trying not to cry. Not because she couldn't seem to admit having achieved her dream goal.

But because of why she couldn't admit it.

What she had with Cade was special. It wasn't a goal or a rescue or a game. It was magic. And even if it was only magic on one side and friendship on the other, or if it lasted a couple of weeks before fading into a glowing memory, it was still hers. It was still special.

She pressed a shaky palm against her churning stomach and tried to take a deep breath through the lump in her throat.

Well, this was a sucky time to realize she was in love with him.

13

"YOU'RE QUIET." CADE'S words were mellow over the gentle hum of the car engine. She could feel his gaze on her but wasn't ready to face her Spring Fling epiphany. "Did I miss something while I was talking to my uncle outside?"

Other than her realizing she was madly in love with him?

"Not much," Eden murmured, finally pulling her gaze from the passing road to look his way. Even in profile, with those gorgeous eyes fixed on the night-blackened road, he was the sexiest man alive.

"You seem a little upset."

Sexiest, and most perceptive.

"I'm just..." Confused, terrified, worried, freaked out. "Overwhelmed."

"By the party? Were the gossips and gawkers a pain?"

For the first time that Eden could remember, the gossips and mean girls had been the least of her woes. Heck, after that scene with Robert, they'd practically been anticlimactic.

Oh, hell. Cade's father.

"Um, something did happen with your father." Eden

winced. "He sort of had an incident while we were talking."

"What kind of an incident?" He shot her a quick look. "Why would you talk to my father? What did he say?"

His father was fresh out of the hospital. So why did he sound more angry than worried? Eden frowned, twisting a little to get a better look at Cade. Wait a second. What was it Robert had said? Between trying to con her into manipulating Cade's career decisions and choking on water? Something about a check?

"Your father's okay," she assured him, despite the lack of concern. "But there was a little incident. Doctor Shaw was right there and took him off to rest."

Brow furrowed, Cade slowed the car to pull into Eden's driveway. He parked in front of the house, but didn't get out. "So that's all? He had an incident? Nothing else?"

"Yep. That's all."

She waited until the tension poured out of him, his fist unclenching from the steering wheel, then added, "Oh, and he mentioned something about you writing a check for me. Something about ten grand?"

Cade cussed under his breath.

"I told him it was taken care of," he muttered. "What the hell, he thinks a country club dance is the place to bring up your mother's debt to him? The man is unreal."

It was like someone sucked all the air out of the car. Eden's chest throbbed and she couldn't catch her breath.

"Seriously?" she asked, her voice a faint whisper. Her mom had taken out *another* loan? How many more were there?

Fury and hurt tangled, making her head throb from the pressure of not screaming.

"Does nobody tell me anything?" she wondered aloud. "Is there some sign over the top of my head claiming I'm incapable of handling the truth? Some notice that was sent around suggesting I be treated like an idiot?"

"You know how Eleanor is," Cade excused, his words rushed, like he was trying to convince her that everything was going to be okay. "She's a little undependable, but I'm sure she intended to take care of everything. Nobody thinks you're an idiot."

"No? Then why didn't you tell me about this added debt?"

Eden didn't wait for Cade's excuse. She was suddenly so mad, she threw open the door and jumped out of the car. Pacing in front of the little porch didn't shake off her fury, so she headed for the wide side yard where she could stomp around freely.

"Wait a second," Cade said as he caught up to her. That he had to shorten his step to keep pace with hers only irritated her more. Eden wanted him panting, struggling to chase her down. Instead it was darned near a leisurely stroll for him. Which pretty much typified everything about their relationship, she realized.

"You aren't blaming me for this?"

"Blaming you for having vital information about my financial situation, and not telling me? Blaming you for knowing that my mother made yet another horrible judgment call that could affect my business and home, but not give me a heads up so I could make sure it's the last one she does? Blaming you for writing a ten-thousand-dollar check…" She was so mad now, she couldn't even walk. Eden stopped and poked her finger at Cade like she was drilling the words home. "To bail me out instead of trusting me to handle the situation myself?"

"Look, you had enough going on, trying to pay off your mom's first loan, keeping up with all the new business. Nosy busybodies. Stuff like that." For just a second, he looked defensive. Like an argument was right there on the tip of his tongue. But then he lifted both palms as if to say he gave up. "I was just trying to help."

Eden's heart, still reeling from the shock of facing her love for him, wept a little.

He was so sweet. So special.

Unable to stop herself, she reached up with both hands and cupped his cheeks, then stood on her tiptoes to brush a kiss over his lips.

"You're just about the sweetest guy in the world," she declared, loving him even more. "But you always do this, Cade. You treat me like I can't take care of myself. I'm not a rescue mission. I'm not the perpetual victim, just here to help you earn your hero badge."

"I'm not using you to get a hero badge," he muttered. "And you're not a victim."

"Oh, let's see. There were three tree rescues, a flat tire, an invitation to the Spring Fling, the two times you got me out of lousy dates and then there is the infamous naked Kenny rescue," Eden said, ticking the items off. "Shall I keep going?"

Cade stood there, moonlight glinting off his navy whites, looking like she'd just bitched him out for rescuing her kittens from a burning building.

"I think you're overreacting just a little bit here. I've never seen you as a victim."

What had he seen her as, then? The girl next door, always there waiting whenever he came home? Did he see her as a temporary fling, the same as she'd tried to convince herself she saw him? Of course, she'd thought that temporary was at least a month. Not two weeks.

"You didn't even tell me you were leaving," she blurted out. Then, slapping both hands over her mouth, Eden groaned, turned on her heel and spun away. Oh, hell. Why had she said that? She had a good reason to be mad. Why was she throwing sad in there, too?

"How'd you find out?"

The anger and defensiveness were gone from Cade's tone now. Instead, he sounded sorry. Tired, even.

"Does it matter?" she asked, turning back to face him. Outing his father for the second time wasn't going to do anybody any good. "Why couldn't you tell me yourself?"

He shrugged, grimacing. "I didn't want to upset you."

"Another rescue?" she whispered, wanting to cry. Again, he was trying to save her. Even from herself. Did he see her as that needy? That pathetic? How could she think they had a chance of being more than just a fantasy if he didn't see her as an equal?

Maybe that was the real fantasy, Eden realized, trying not to cry. Believing that she and Cade actually had a chance.

"Come to San Diego," he said all of a sudden.

Still wallowing in the heartache, Eden frowned, then shook her head. "What? To visit? Shouldn't you wait until you're back, see where you're assigned?"

In the time they'd been together, he'd never talked about his missions, hadn't mentioned any locales or places he'd been. Other than describing the physical training he did on a regular basis, he hadn't referenced his job at all. But she knew from his grandmother that Cade was often outside of the U.S. for months at a time.

"Sure. I'm thinking about a transfer. Out of SEALs, into the training program. I'd be one of those hard-ass drill sergeant types, molding the next wave of SEALs. It'd mean no more travel." He hesitated, his face a study of doubt. Then he gave a shrug. "Maybe I could get an apartment instead of living on base. You could come, stay with me."

Joy and shock tangled with a dozen other emotions, all rushing through Eden like a hurricane.

"Why would you do that? Why would you leave the SEALs?"

"I'm not happy," he said simply. "Something's missing. Something vital."

"But to leave the SEALs? Are you sure you want to take that big of a step? Maybe you're just suffering from burnout. We all hit it once in a while. I'll bet you just need a little more time off," she suggested. *Maybe a month or so, right here in Ocean Point.*

"Lives depend on me, Eden. On me being one-hundred percent. If I can't give that, I shouldn't be leading. Shouldn't be on the team." He walked over to the paddock, staring across the land toward his father's house. "I figure I'll give training a try, see how that goes. See if I still have a career with the navy."

He sounded so sad.

But when he turned to face her, he wore his usual charming smile. "And, hey, now we have a chance. The odds of things working out if I'm a SEAL are slim to none. But this way, we can see where things go. You can visit me in San Diego. I can come up here. What do you think?"

What did she think?

Eden pressed her hand against her churning stomach.

She thought it was an incredible idea.

To see if this heat between them could last, could grow. She thought it'd be so much easier knowing that Cade was safe.

This was so much bigger than her birthday wish fantasy. So much more than she'd ever let herself hope she'd have with Cade.

He valued her enough to base the biggest decision of his life on her opinion. All it would take was one word from her and he'd take a safer job. One that'd keep him in one place for long periods of time. One that would give them a chance.

Eden had spent so much of her life wanting to be special to someone. Special enough that she'd matter so much that her opinion, her feelings mattered.

It felt as if she was teetering on the edge of that now. This thing, the heat and laughter and comfortable joy between her and Cade, it was special. It could be more. It could be everything she'd ever dreamed of.

All she had to do was tell him to leave the SEALs. But he was using her, using this career choice, as a way to hide. To avoid dealing with the pain of losing his friend. Eden knew Cade well enough to read between the lines. In his mind, the only way they could stay together was if he left the SEALs.

But if he left, he'd never heal.

All her life, she'd wanted to be special. To be wanted, just for her. To belong.

Now, when she'd finally found the one person who made her feel that way, she was thinking about sending him away.

"You need to ask yourself what it is you really want," she said quietly. "Don't think about your father. Don't think about Phil. Don't even think about me. Just focus on you."

Cade shook his head, as if that was an impossible request. Eden took a deep breath, blinking fast to clear the hot tears from her eyes.

She turned away, staring at the small barn that housed her clinic. Her dream.

Years of watching Cade, of being rescued by him, of obsessing and fantasizing about him gave her a strong insight. She knew this man inside out. She knew what made him smile, and now she knew what made him groan with pleasure. She knew his likes and dislikes, his fetishes and, her heart sighed, she knew his fears.

She knew exactly why he was talking about giving up his career. And it had nothing to do with her.

And everything to do with him.

So, for the first time in their lives, she was going to turn the table.

This time, she was going to rescue Cade.

And then she was going to crawl into bed and cry for a month.

"Look, you'd really like San Diego," Cade said, talking to Eden's back. His words were edgy, a little desperate, but dammit, she wasn't reacting the way he'd hoped. Hell, he'd just tossed relationship promises out there and she hadn't jumped in to grab a single one of them. "I'll introduce you to Alexia, Blake's fiancée. You'll like her. She's an animal kind of gal."

Actually he couldn't remember if Alexia liked animals or not. He could barely remember his name after that chat with Seth. His uncle was worried. Afraid Cade was pushing himself too hard. He'd been the one to put the idea in Cade's head that Eden come to San Diego. But as soon as the thought was there, Cade couldn't get it out. He wanted it, wanted her.

And she was acting like she wasn't even interested.

Damn, tonight sucked.

Finally Eden turned around. Her face was set, chin high and shoulders pulled back. What the hell? He'd seen enough people prepare for battle to recognize that look.

"You are so wonderful." Her eyes were clear as she stared up at him, but Cade had the feeling there were tears behind them somewhere. Why, though? This was good, right? They were talking about their future, making big plans. Didn't women love that kind of thing?

"So why don't you sound like you want to be into wonderful?" he asked. His tone was teasing, but he didn't stop searching her face for clues.

"This thing—" she gestured with her fingers between them "—between us... Cade, it was just for fun. You know, a good time."

"Yeah, we did have a good time. But we had more than that, too." Poor thing, she was so used to dating idiots like that Kenny that she probably didn't realize she was making her declaration sound like a prelude to dumping him.

"No." Eden shook her head, her eyes sad now. Shuttered. Like she was pushing him away. "That's all we had. Fun. A fantasy. A birthday wish, remember?"

"What's between us is bigger than just a fantasy," he protested.

They had laughter. They had passion and joy and a connection that went deep. They understood each other. And dammit, they comforted each other. He found peace when he was with Eden. The nightmares didn't ache when he woke to find her face on the pillow next to him. He could shove aside the memories just by focusing on her, on how she made him feel.

Cade stared down at Eden's closed expression. Her lush lashes cast a shadow on pale cheeks, silky hair fell in soft curls around a face he knew as well as his own.

He didn't know when it had happened. Maybe this week. Maybe years ago. But he loved her.

Simply loved her.

That was what they had between them.

"Look..." Suddenly nervous, he tried to gather the words. He'd never told a woman he loved her before, so they weren't coming easily.

As if she knew he was about to make a major declaration, she backed away shaking her head. Cade grabbed her hands to pull her back.

"No," she said again. She gave him a look that made him feel like he'd crushed her heart. "No, Cade. We were really good together. But that's not enough to make it long term. It's not something you leave your job for. You don't quit a career you love for a good time."

Spine stiff against the accusation that he was quitting, Cade ground his teeth together to keep from arguing. After all, maybe, for her a good time was all they were?

"Is it my job? The risks?" He saw something flash in her eyes, enough that he figured he'd nailed the issue. Taking a deep breath, a part of him feeling like the quitter his father always declared he was while the rest was thrilled not to have to think about it anymore, Cade declared, "Don't let that be a problem, okay? Like I said, I'll be changing positions. There's not much danger in yelling at recruits."

"You won't be happy walking away from the SEALs, Cade," she told him, her words certain.

Since a part of him was currently doing backflips over the idea, Cade had no problem disagreeing. "I think I know what I want, Eden."

"And I know what will make you happy. I know you inside out, Cade. You, the man."

Cade didn't know why he suddenly wanted to leave. To be done with this conversation. But the idea of getting the hell out of there before she revealed any of the truths in her eyes was so freaking tempting.

"Look, I've got a pretty solid handle on my happiness," he lied. "Nobody knows me better than I know myself."

"The man loves his grandmother," she said, lifting one finger.

Before Cade could point out that description could be

applied to most non-psychopaths, she took a step closer and continued.

"Despite being brought up to be a Class-A snob, the man prefers beer in a bottle and burgers in wrappers to wine and filet mignon." Two fingers and another step closer. Cade was too proud to back up.

"The man is the kind of friend who goes to the edge for people he cares about. One who cares so much, he holds their loss in his heart in order to honor them." Three fingers jabbed the air this time, but Cade could barely see them through his blurred gaze.

His jaw clenched against the barrage of feeling her words brought on. As if she'd opened that memorial he'd created in his heart for Phil and forced him to truly see it.

He was so engrossed in those feelings, he barely noticed that Eden was standing, high-heel-to-boot in front of him now.

"The man is so heartbroken, he's willing to hide from the pain he feels instead of honoring where it came from. To take on a relationship he doesn't want so he can ignore the one he's lost."

It was like getting sucker punched in the gut.

Who the hell was she to rip open the safeguards he'd built around his heart and force him to see what was inside?

"You're a wonderful man, Cade. But you're trying to use what you *think* we have to hide from what's missing in your life. You're trying to turn our little fantasy into something more. To convince yourself it'll be enough to fill the huge, gaping hole that'd be left if you leave the SEALs."

What a bunch of crap. But he was too used to standing up for Eden, to hurrying to her rescue, to say that to her face. But just because he didn't tell her that she was so far off base she was writing fiction, didn't mean he wasn't thinking it.

Even as a part of him wondered if maybe she wasn't just a tiny, little bit right.

"What we have is special," he claimed, focusing on the only part of her argument he was willing to discuss. This was stupid. He wasn't letting her cold feet, or whatever she was dealing with, ruin things between them.

"No," she said, her words so quiet they almost flew away on the gentle evening breeze. "Like I said, we were just a fantasy. A wish."

He could hear her swallow, like the words were a painful lump in her throat, before she continued.

"You came to my rescue, as always. But this time you didn't even realize it. Our relationship got me more attention than anything I could have done on my own. The gossips, the busybodies were so excited about us, they made my business a success. And you, us, this affair—" Her voice broke. Then she lifted her chin and gave him a chilly smile. "This affair guaranteed my social standing in town. So, again, thanks for the rescue."

"What?" No. He couldn't have heard her right. Cade shook his head to try and throw off the buzzing in his ears. She was bullshitting him. There was no way Eden would use him like that.

"I'm a Cade-ette now. I've finally got a secure spot in Ocean Point's social register. I won't have to ever worry again about getting invited to all the right parties. You not only gave me a couple of weeks of incredible sex, Cade. You guaranteed my business would be a success."

All he could do was stand there in the moonlight and stare at her. If she'd pulled a machine gun out from under her dress and opened fire, he couldn't have been more shocked.

But she didn't pull anything out. She just gave him a long, sad look, then turned on her fancy high heels and walked toward her house.

Cade just stood there, watching.

She never looked back.

He wanted to yell.

To punch something. To attack. To fight.

Cade wasn't sure he'd ever felt as betrayed as he did in that second. He knew he'd never been as hurt.

Fists clenched at his side, he wanted to grab onto the fury, to revel in the anger. But the pain was so much stronger. He couldn't use anger to hide from it, because Eden had never promised him any more than sex. She'd never indicated that she was fishing for a ring.

Nope, right from the get go, that night on the cliffs, she'd said she wanted the fantasy.

Could he blame her that she was willing to let the fantasy do double duty? To give her both pleasure, and a little security?

Still, not even losing Phil had made him feel this miserable.

He'd listened to Seth tonight as his uncle outlined all of the reasons why Cade should give the SEALs a break. The only point his uncle hadn't made was that Cade had lost his edge when Phil had died in combat.

Because that was the only point that really mattered.

The one Eden had beat him in the gut with.

He wanted to go after her. To tell her she was right. That he needed to heal, but didn't know how.

Except Eden didn't care about that.

She'd gotten what she wanted.

She'd gotten her fantasy wish. A whole lot of good sex, and a Cade-ette T-shirt.

Instead of following her, though, he slowly made his way to his car.

As he started the ignition, he congratulated himself.

He should be happy. He'd escaped a potential nightmare. Changing his career, just for Eden? To give them a chance at a future?

What a mistake that would have been, given that there wasn't any.

At last, not to Eden.

14

SHE SHOULD BE DOING BACKFLIPS.

Yesterday, she'd met with Mia Warren about trying out a partnership. Mia had an extensive client list, but no physical clinic to operate out of since the old vet she'd worked with had retired last year. Eden would get access to those clients, in exchange for Mia using the clinic one day a week. There were still a lot of details to discuss, but, so far, it was sounding like a dream come true.

She'd fielded four phone calls, happily turning down two requests that she serve on committees, had blown off Kenny Phillips's offer of drinks and dinner sometime, and had accepted Crystal's invitation to go shopping, on the condition that Bev join them.

And she'd only thought of Cade, oh, a million miserable times.

Not bad for a day spent wishing she was curled up in her bed, the covers drawn comfortably over her head. That, or cozied up in McCall's Bakery stuffing herself with chocolate fudge muffins, apple fritters and cheesecake brownies.

This pain would go away. The heartbreak, the misery, they'd fade. Eden figured if she kept promising herself that, sooner or later she'd buy into the hype and start believing it.

In the meantime, she'd just keep on moving forward. Enjoy the blessings that were rolling into her life. All she'd had to do to bring in all of those blessings was get that first wish out of the way, and then it'd snowballed. It had broken her heart, too, of course. She really shouldn't forget that part of the equation.

But she was determined not to let it turn her into a whiny baby who hid her chocolate-smeared face under her pillow.

Her determination to keep that from happening was the reason she was here at the Oceanfront Country Club. She trudged across the parquet floor on her favorite pair of perky and cheerful ballet flats, wondering why Catherine had called this morning, insisting she come to breakfast.

"Eden, darling."

Reluctantly pulled out of her reverie, Eden looked around. A genuine smile curved her mouth when she saw Mrs. Carmichael floating toward her in a brilliant blue caftan and earrings the size of gold dinner plates.

"Good morning." Eden's greeting ended in a surprised squeak when the older woman engulfed her in a hug.

"You are a miracle worker, my dear. My Paisley has never looked better. Those supplements and the diet changes you recommended are wonderful."

"I'm so glad. You'll have to bring her in to see Mooch again. I've never seen him take to a cat the way he did Paisley."

"That's exactly what I wanted to talk to you about. Adopting Mooch."

"But I thought Mr. Carmichael is allergic to dogs." Trying not to get too excited, Eden shook her head. "I want

Mooch to have a loving home, but not at the expense of your husband's comfort."

"Pshaw, I think he's more allergic to walking a dog than anything else. But, it won't be my house Mooch will live in. My niece, Kelly, moved back to town. She wants a pet and he'd be perfect." Mrs. Carmichael gave Eden a narrow look, then added, "Kelly's about your age, dear. You come to lunch next week, and the two of you can get to know each other. You'll be good for her. You can introduce her around, help her settle in."

"Me?" Shocked, Eden shook her head again. "Don't you want someone more, you know, in with the right crowd?"

"What? One of those society leeches like Janie Truman? That girl and the ones in her circle, they are all takers. You're a sweet girl. You help, contribute, make a difference." With that and a pat of her chubby hand on Eden's shoulder, Mrs. Carmichael turned to leave. "We'll have lunch on Wednesday at my house. Bring Mooch, please."

Eden could only blink a few times and try to process that while watching the other woman float away. Well, look at that. More good news.

She wished she could be excited.

Sighing, she approached the hostess station.

"I'm meeting Mrs. Sullivan," Eden told the woman.

The pretty redhead leaned forward to give Eden a big smile. "I'm so glad to see you. I was going to call this afternoon when I get off shift."

"I beg your pardon?"

"My cat had kittens. Under the front porch, no less. One of them is tiny. I'm kind of worried and was hoping I could make an appointment to bring them all in to see you. I know it's short notice, but maybe today or tomorrow?"

Eden blinked a couple of times, wondering if she'd heard right. "You want to bring your cats in to see me?"

"Is that okay?"

She should be excited. Business was great, everything was working out. Instead, she wanted to cry.

Keeping her chin stiff, she said, "Of course. Why don't you bring them by anytime tomorrow?"

"Awesome," the hostess said with a grateful smile as she came around the podium and gestured toward the dining room.

Eden followed her through the crowded tables, smiling at a few faces here and there. It was like walking through a sea of whispers. She heard her name, and Cade's, at least a dozen times. The gossip never ended. That would follow her, an ever-present reminder of the cost of having her wish. A part of her wanted it to go away. But that'd mean giving up her time with Cade. And even though it had ended, even though her heart felt like it had shattered in two, she couldn't wish that time away.

Blinking away tears, she was so focused on not breaking down, she didn't see the other two people sitting with Catherine Sullivan until she reached the table.

Shock rocked her back so far, she was glad she was wearing flats instead of heels. Otherwise she'd have landed on her butt.

"Mr. Sullivan," she greeted quietly, wincing at the slight gray cast to his skin. Obviously he still hadn't quite recovered from his encounter with the glass of water the other night. And if his steely stare was any indication, he hadn't forgiven her for it, either.

No matter. It was obviously going to be a non-forgiving kind of get-together, she decided as she shifted her gaze to the third person at the table.

Fury, frustration and a surge of love all twined together as Eden lifted her chin and in her chilliest tone greeted, "Hello, Mother."

As far as parents went, Eleanor was a stunner. Traveling across the country had clearly agreed with the woman, who glowed like she'd just had a luxury spa treatment.

"Darling, it's so good to see you." Eleanor made as if to get up and offer her only child a hug, but Eden wasn't having any of that. She quickly slid into the chair next to Catherine instead, so her mother had to settle for patting her hand.

"You must be surprised," Catherine said in a gentle tone. She gave Eden a sympathetic look from those eyes so like Cade's and smiled. "I was afraid if I told you who would be joining us, you might find an excuse to refuse breakfast."

"I never refuse breakfast," she said with the closest thing to a smile she could muster. "Actually, breakfast is my favorite meal. I'm especially fond of the stuffed French toast they make here. That, and the breakfast biscuits. They're as flaky as they are light."

"Eden—"

Eden's jaw clenched. Before she could snap, Catherine sent Eleanor a chiding look, then gestured for Eden to continue.

"Speaking of breakfast," Eden added, after taking a deep breath. "The special-blend kibble you ordered for Alfie arrived yesterday. I have it in my car to give to you before we leave."

"Alfie will love that, dear." Catherine took a sip of her tea, then launched a soliloquy on the wonderfulness that was her new pet.

In the next five minutes, Eden discovered three things. Robert Sullivan hated being ignored. He looked like he was about to burst, his face was so red and tight. And she wasn't sure how much longer her mother could go without saying a word, but she was impressed that Eleanor's upbringing was so solidly ingrained that she managed to keep her friendly smile in place, even while she wore her fingernails down tapping them on the table.

But best of all, she realized that Catherine was a total imp. The society matron knew perfectly well that she was torturing her son and driving her guest crazy, but from the way her eyes were dancing, she didn't care. All she seemed focused on was talking about her sweet little Yorkie.

And, Eden realized, putting her at her ease.

Almost moved to grateful tears, Eden decided she'd taken advantage of the older woman's machinations long enough. She took a deep breath, then offered a hesitant smile.

"Mrs. Sullivan, I have to apologize for leaving the Spring Fling early. I wasn't feeling my best. But that's no excuse for my rudeness in not staying to help out."

As if she'd been waiting for Eden to get to that point, Catherine nodded, then gestured to the other two people scowling at the table.

"You shouldn't feel bad for needing to leave, dear," she chided. "From what I understand, my son was horribly uncouth, tactlessly discussing matters that had no business being mentioned at a social event."

Eden's lips twitched when Robert actually hung his head at that, still frowning despite his abashed look.

Since there was nothing she could say to top that chastisement, she turned her attention to her mother instead.

"I've been trying to reach you for two weeks. What made you finally decide to come home?" she asked, trying to keep her tone neutral but afraid it still had a strong layer of bitterness on top.

"Cade reached me in Connecticut yesterday. He insisted I return." Eleanor leaned forward and, ignoring Eden's glare, took both of her daughter's hands. "Oh, darling, I'm

sorry. I didn't mean to be so out of touch. I'd met a wonderful couple at my first craft fair who suggested I try the
eastern circuit instead of the southern route. Oh, sweetie,
it was wonderful. My erotic pottery was a huge hit. Then
I got so distracted with the shows, the new people, that I
totally forgot about checking in with you."

No surprise there. Eden's anger, fueled by the hurt of
always being forgotten by her own mother, faded a little.
It was hard to hold a grudge against Eleanor for simply
being her usual self-absorbed self. Still, she'd gone behind Eden's back, borrowed against the house, then ran
out on her debts.

"I tried calling you, Mother. I left a dozen or more mes-
sages. You never returned any of them."

"I forgot to charge that silly phone."

"Then how did Cade—" Eden paused to swallow the
lump in her throat. It even hurt to say his name. "How did
he reach you?"

"He had me arrested."

Robert's snort drowned out the sound of Eden's gasp.

"Arrested?"

"Well, I guess that's what you'd call it." Sunlight glistened off the dozen rings on Eleanor's fingers as she waved
her hand. "I was picked up by the military police in Gro-
ton."

Eden narrowed her eyes, then shook her head. "You
don't seem very upset for someone who was detained,
Mother."

"Well, the boy who stopped me *was* very cute. And so
polite. What a lovely credit to the navy he was. Much like
Cade, of course," Eleanor said, giving both Catherine and
Robert a bright smile. "What a sweet man he's grown to
be. As angry as he had to be, he sent his uncle to meet me

at the airport and bring me here in time to meet with the three of you."

Cade had arranged this. He'd tracked down her flake of a mother, called in military favors and made all these arrangements. He really was her hero.

"I didn't mean to get you into this mess, Sweetie. I simply lost track of time and forgot the payments were due."

"Speaking of payments, I have a proposition for you and your mother," Robert interrupted, pulling her attention back to the less friendly faces at her own table.

"What's that?" Eden asked, not caring since she knew anything he proposed wasn't going to be in her favor. Still, she couldn't be rude with Catherine sitting right there.

"You use your influence on my son. Convince him not to take this new assignment." Robert reached into the pocket of his suit jacket and pulled out a check. The one Cade had written for ten thousand dollars, Eden realized. "You do that, and I'll forgive your mother's loan. You want to help your mom, don't you?"

Eden's mouth dropped. She didn't know what was worse. That he would try to bribe her to con his own son, or that he thought she would consider it.

Before she could say anything, or even try to talk over the strident scolding Catherine was serving up, her mother interrupted.

"Oh, now that's just silly. Eden isn't responsible for my debts. Robert, I told you that I'd pay you. Time just got away from me."

"The loan was due last month, and you missed that deadline. Now we're discussing new terms."

"Robert," Catherine whispered, her face a study of anger.

"Don't be silly. The terms we agreed on are just fine," Eleanor said with a flutter of her lashes. "Even though you didn't cash that check from Cade yet, taking it was implicit acceptance of payment, after all. I'd planned to give the cash directly to him, but this is easier."

Eleanor leaned over to lift a suede bag from her feet, setting it on the table with a dull thud. She tugged open the drawstrings, and the fabric fell away, revealing a foot-tall pottery sculpture with a pile of neatly bundled bills at its feet.

Eden knew she should be gaping at all of those dollars. Ten thousand of them at least, she figured. But it was hard to tear her eyes off the vivid pink color and distinctive shape.

"What the…"

"That's a little bonus. A sort of thank you for being so patient," Eleanor told him, giving the large ceramic vulva one last proud pat. "It's part of my Evolving Woman series. I have other pieces if you'd like a different color."

"You've got to be kidding," Robert protested. "What are you doing, making that, that…?"

"This is art. I used to call it a craft. And then I did this little trip and learned the difference. I, my dears, create art," Eleanor declared. "Art that earns me a tidy bundle. Enough to pay you back, pay off the bank and repay my sweet Eden. You should learn to expand your horizons a little, Robert."

"Expand my…?"

Eden's lips twitched. The man was actually speechless.

"We should always be true to ourselves, after all. Look at my Eden, here. She's worked hard to follow her dreams. Going to school all those years, getting her degree and coming back to open her veterinary clinic here." Eleanor's smile beamed across the table, warming her daughter. "And your Cade. You must be so proud of him, of all he's done. Not because he's a SEAL, but because he's followed his dream. Because he's been true to himself. That's all we want as parents, isn't it?"

Eden was so busy doing an emotional tailspin, she missed the rest of her mother's lecture on parenting from the heart.

She *had* followed her dreams. She was seeing her wishes come true and even more dreams manifest. She didn't know if it was because she'd been so excited, so confident and empowered after she got her wish for fantasy sex with Cade. Whatever it was, she'd been making her own decisions all along. She'd chosen to have sex with Cade. She'd been the one to maneuver all the gossips into bringing in their pets if they wanted to be nosy. Right up until the Spring Fling, when she'd elected to walk away from Janie's taunts instead of using her relationship to gain a coveted spot as a Cade-ette.

Suddenly feeling a little ill, Eden gulped iced lemon water and tried to pretend her mother wasn't petting ceramic girly bits.

She'd made all those choices.

But she hadn't let Cade make his own decision.

She'd tried to rescue him.

Instead of letting him rescue himself.

Exactly what she'd accused him of doing.

Eden's heart sank.

Even if she'd ruined things between her and Cade, she had to fix her mistake.

Eden got to her feet so fast, the ceramic vulva teetered. Eleanor gasped and grabbed the statue. Robert growled. Catherine gave a serene smile.

"Mr. Sullivan, please take my mother's payment and consider this matter closed." Eden interrupted his stutters and leaned across the table, giving him a stern look. "And consider this. You are lucky to have a son as wonderful as

yours. If you want a little advice, you might start appreciating what you have. If you want something from Cade, talk
to him. Be truthful. These silly games are beneath you."

Advice she'd do well to listen to herself.

With that, and a quick kiss for both Catherine and her
grinning mother, Eden turned on the heel of her very practical shoes and glided from the room.

It was, if she did say so herself, the most graceful exit
of her life.

CADE STUMBLED DOWN the stairs, wincing as the bright sunlight pierced his sleep-deprived eyes, and felt his way into
the kitchen. Who the hell was making all this noise?

His grandmother's rules drilled into his head, he auto-
matically pasted on a smile filled with as much charm as
he could muster with a hangover and yanked open the door.

As soon as he saw who was on the other side, his smile
dropped, along with his mood—which hadn't been too
perky to begin with.

"What? You need an affidavit signed stating you qualify for the Cade-ettes?" he asked, leaning his bare shoulder against the doorframe and giving Eden a distant look.

"Clever." Eden gave him a shaky smile that fell away
quickly when he didn't smile back.

She looked so damned good. Her hair was slicked back
in a tidy braid, her face glowing in the morning light. There
wasn't a hint of misery or even a smidge of a hangover in
her big brown eyes.

Damn her.

"Can I come in?"

"Why? Catherine isn't here."

There. He wanted her to leave, that should do it. Cade
steeled himself against the hurt he expected to see on her

face. But Eden lifted her chin and gave him a look that said she was more determined than dissuaded. *What the hell?*

"I need to talk to you." She bit her lip, then offered a big, bright smile. "I need your help."

Cade's jaw dropped.

"You're kidding, right?"

She was kidding, right?

Instead of assuring him that this was a joke, Eden brushed past, gave his arm a quick pat, then hurried into the sitting room.

Cade wanted to believe it was shocked curiosity that had him following and not the fact that, even now, he couldn't refuse her a single thing.

"You need my help?" he repeated, trying to smother his automatic call to action. "With what?"

Seating herself on his grandmother's antique settee, Eden opened her mouth to respond, then her eyes went wide and hot. Cade glanced down and grimaced, realizing he'd stormed down the stairs in just a pair of jeans. He should excuse himself and put a shirt on at least.

But he liked that look on her face. He watched her eyes heat as they trailed over his body like a hot caress. He liked the way she wet her bottom lip and took a deep breath, as if the sight of him was a total turn-on.

It didn't matter that they were through, or that she'd used him. He couldn't stop his body's reaction.

"What do you need help with?" he asked again, wanting her eyes back on his face before his body's reaction became any more apparent.

"What?" She blinked a couple of times, then puffed out a breath. "Oh. Right. Um, first, before we get into that, I wanted to say thank you."

"For what?"

For getting her into an exclusive club?

For giving her two weeks of mind-blowing sex?

For falling crazy in love with her?

"For hauling my mother home. Making her face her responsibilities and take care of the mess she'd left." Eden looked down at her knees for a second, as if smothering a smile. "She paid your father this morning, and is meeting with the bank manager this afternoon. So thank you, yet again, for rescuing me."

Cade frowned. He hadn't pickled his brain so much that he'd forgotten her accusations just two days ago. That he saw her as a perpetual victim, that he didn't believe she could take care of herself. She'd yelled at him for rescuing her all the time. And now she was thanking him for it?

He rubbed at the throbbing pain in his temple. What was she trying to do?

"I don't get it," he confessed. "Now you're glad I rescued you?"

"Yes." She said the word so fast it was practically a rush of air. Then she bit her lip again and gave him one of those sweet, big-eyed stares.

"Why?"

"Because I realized that it's not a judgment or sign that you don't respect me. It's proof that you care. A way of trying to help. Of stepping in to keep me from getting hurt."

Right.

His frown deepened. He narrowed his gaze.

"What are you up to?"

Eden jumped up from the couch and started pacing. Fireplace to window, chair to piano. After two rounds, she took a deep breath and met his gaze.

"I sort of have something to confess."

Did she want to confess that she really cared about him? Admit that she was miserable without him?

Beg him to strip her naked and do wild and naughty things to her body?

From the scared look on her face, Cade figured it was probably none of the above.

"I sort of didn't tell you the truth the other night," she said, her words murmured to her toes instead of his face.

"I beg your pardon?"

Even after she'd told him she'd used him to get into that stupid club, Cade didn't think Eden had it in her to actually lie.

"I didn't really try to get into the Cade-ettes. I refused to tell Janie what we had between us."

"Then why'd you say you did?"

"I was afraid you were going to throw your career away. That you'd make this huge decision and regret it later. I figured if you didn't have me as an excuse, you'd stick with the SEALs until you really knew if you wanted to leave or not."

Cade's mind reeled. But one clear fact stood out in the spinning confusion.

"You were trying to rescue me?"

Her smile was half-grimace, half-wince.

"I was afraid you'd give up something you loved for the wrong reason."

"You think leaving the SEALs for you is the wrong reason?"

"I think leaving the SEALs because you can't get over the loss of your friend is the wrong reason," she said gently, lifting his grandmother's framed photo of him, Blake and Phil graduating bootcamp.

Cade stared at the picture.

It was like he was at war with himself.

A part of him was tired. Just so damned tired. A year would give him time to decide if he wanted to stick with the SEALs or shift focus. It would give him time to get past the loss of Phil, to process his feelings about command. To heal.

Damned if he'd even known he was wounded until Eden made him face the truth. Just like he wouldn't have realized he was in love with her until she'd walked out on him.

The real question wasn't what he was going to do about his job. The question on the table right now was what was he going to do about his life.

"You were right," he finally said.

"I was…?"

"Right," he repeated. Cade shoved both hands through his hair, then shrugged. "I wanted to use you to avoid making a choice. To avoid admitting that I might want to do something other than be a SEAL."

"And now?" Her words were whisper soft, but so loaded with understanding that Cade felt as if she'd come over and wrapped him in a big hug.

"And now I know what I'm going to do. Just like I know I need to quit hiding and face the loss of my buddy." It hurt to say the words. To admit that he was ready to take that first step toward healing. It'd be like saying goodbye to Phil all over again. But he couldn't have a future if he was stuck in the past.

He looked at Eden, and knew.

He wanted to make her his future.

EDEN WAS SO GLAD she hadn't stayed at the country club long enough to actually eat anything, because her stomach was doing all sorts of crazy backflips.

All her life, she'd wished for more. She'd blown out candles and watched for falling stars. She'd dreamed of what it'd be like to have her perfect life.

But today, she'd finally realized that all the wishing

in the world didn't matter. It was the doing that made the difference.

And she really, really loved doing Cade.

She took a deep breath, knowing she needed to confess everything before she lost her nerve. Or jumped his body. Her eyes ran over the sleek silken glow of his muscles again and her mouth started to water. The odds of both things happening were running pretty even at that moment.

"What you said the other night made me realize that I've spent years sitting idly by, waiting. Hoping that if I was good enough, nice enough, that everyone, someone, *anyone* would see that I was worthy."

He looked like he wanted to argue as if the idea of her thinking that she was less than perfect simply pissed him off. Eden loved that about him. Loved how strongly he wanted to defend her.

"But you always saw me as worthy. Even when you hauled me out of trees or kept me from falling on my face, you made me feel like I was special. Even when all there was between us was a mutual street sign and a lot of rescues, you accepted me. So, now I'm through waiting," she said, her heart pounding so loud she wouldn't have been surprised if he could hear it. But it was beating with excitement, rather than fear. Because even if he turned her down, she'd have tried. She'd have given them her best shot.

"What're you through waiting for?" he asked slowly. Clearly his training had clued him in that he might be in danger.

"I'm through waiting for all of my wishes to come true." Eden took a deep breath, then walked over until she stood in front of him. Her fingers ached to touch, but she kept them at her sides.

"I realized today that I do make things happen. I made the right choices that led to opportunities, or the lack thereof. I might need to be rescued once in a while because I'm chasing the dream. But that's okay, because I'm the one choosing to run after it," she whispered.

His eyes gleamed, the smile starting to play at the corners of his mouth giving her a little encouragement.

"So what're you planning to make happen next?"

"This," she told him, launching herself into his waiting arms. Both hands cupping his cheeks, she ravaged his mouth. Cade, gentleman that he was, ravaged her right back.

"I love you," she breathed against his mouth. For a split second, she wanted to grab the words back. To wait and see if he said them first. Then she lifted her chin and met his eyes. Nope. No waiting. Not any longer.

"I love you," she repeated, her words strong and sure this time. "I want to give us a chance. I'll spend time in San Diego, whether it's once a year when you're on leave or a few times a month if you're doing training. Whatever you decide, for whatever reasons you see fit, I want to be there for you."

For just a second, he looked shocked. Then a smile like she'd never seen—one filled with little-boy joy, delight and hope—split his face.

"I'd say we have one hell of a chance," he decided, sweeping her into his arms and carrying her to the couch where he settled with her tight in his arms. "Because I love you, too."

Eden was pretty sure her heart stopped.

She stared, wide-eyed, for two breaths until it started again. Elation surged as she met his lips, their kiss as raw and honest as their declarations of love.

"Looks like my birthday wish came true," she said when they came up for air.

"Yeah? The one about us having a lot of sex?" He pulled

her more firmly onto his lap, the hard length of his erection pressing against her thigh, letting her know he couldn't wait to start.

"I do like that part," she agreed with a laugh, wriggling just a little to tease him. "But the part I've always wished for, even before sex with you, was to have my very own hero."

Cade's smile softened, his eyes warming hers as he pressed a kiss of promise against her lips.

"I'll always be your hero."

Epilogue

CADE LAY ON THE BED, his hands crossed behind his head while he contemplated just how damned great his life was. It had been nine months since the infamous Spring Fling and he and Eden were as strong as ever together.

So strong, he actually believed in taking chances now instead of following the tried and true. In his jacket pocket was his mother's engagement ring. His father had suggested he use it when he'd told Robert and Catherine that he was asking Eden to marry him.

Nerves danced for a second while he tried to decide how to ask. She'd say yes, wouldn't she? Thanks to her partnership with Mia, she'd changed her veterinary schedule to spend a week or two each month with him in San Diego. He spent all of his breaks between training sessions here in Ocean Point with her. She'd even started working with pet-placement groups in Southern California. Those were good signs, right?

The nerves in his belly got a little more active.

"Blake and Alexia should be back from their honeymoon next week," he said, grateful for the distraction when Eden stepped out of the bathroom, steam from her shower billowing around her. "You up for a week or two in San Diego? We'll take them out to celebrate married life."

"Maybe."

He frowned in surprise at her response. Eden and Alexia had become pretty good friends. In fact, within a week of meeting her, Alexia had adjusted her wedding plans to include Eden as a bridesmaid.

So what was up?

Eden stopped at the foot of the bed, her worried frown driving everything from his mind.

"What's wrong?" he asked, jackknifing into a sitting position. He knew her face, her every expression. She was scared. Anxious and happy all at the same time.

What the hell?

"Um, well, I think I— We broke something."

Cade looked around. No damage.

He shifted to take in her body, from the top of her silky brown hair, over the tiny red nightie and down to the tips of her pale pink toes.

"What?"

Eden bit her lip, then, with the soft flesh still tight between her teeth, she held out a stick.

Cade looked at it, frowned and gave a shrug.

"What's that?"

"It's, um, a pregnancy test."

What? Cade's gaze flew from the stick to her face and back again. Then it landed on her stomach, flat as ever under her silky nightgown.

"A condom broke?" he confirmed in an awed tone.

Wincing, she gave a little shrug, then nodded.

He threw back his head and laughed.

God, could life get any better?

Loving it, loving her, he leaped from the bed and swept Eden into his arms to spin her in a wide circle. On his second time around, he grabbed his jacket in one hand then dropped to the bed with Eden in his lap.

"Talk about accident prone," she muttered.

"Babe, this isn't an accident. This is a blessing, pure and simple."

To prove it to her, he scooped the little velvet box out of the pocket, letting the jacket fall to the floor as he flipped the lid and held out the diamond.

Eden's eyes widened, then went soft with so much love that Cade had to blink.

"Will you marry me?"

"Did you already know I was pregnant?" she asked in shock, reaching out to touch the ring with one unsteady finger before pulling her hand back.

"Nope. I knew I loved you. I knew I wanted to spend the rest of my life with you." Cade caught her hand in his, brought it to his lips and brushed a kiss over her knuckles before twining his fingers with hers. "You being pregnant only adds to the perfection we've got together. It's like a sign that I'm making all the right choices, that I'm living my life for my own dreams instead of trying to prove something to my father. Something to myself."

Eden's smile was a little shaky at the corners.

"I don't expect you to give up being a SEAL. I know the BUDs training was just a temporary thing. I don't want you to think you have to give up going back into Special Ops."

Cade had to close his eyes for a second, he was so overcome by emotions. She was incredible.

"Babe, I love training. It's like I was made for it. I love being stationary, able to come home to you every night. I love the idea of building a life together, of bringing a new life into the world with you." He watched the worry fade from her dark gaze, then slid the ring on her finger before kissing her with all the love and passion he had in his heart.

When she was breathless and limp, he pulled back to give her his most charming smile. "Bottom line, I love you."

Eden's laugh was so soft, it was more a puff of breath over his face than a sound. She cupped his face in both hands and kissed him again.

"My hero."

* * * * *

REQUEST YOUR FREE BOOKS!
2 FREE NOVELS PLUS 2 FREE GIFTS!

HARLEQUIN®

Blaze®

red-hot reads!

YES! Please send me 2 FREE Harlequin® Blaze™ novels and my 2 FREE gifts (gifts are worth about $10). After receiving them, if I don't wish to receive any more books, I can return the shipping statement marked "cancel." If I don't cancel, I will receive 4 brand-new novels every month and be billed just $4.49 per book in the U.S. or $4.96 per book in Canada. That's a savings of at least 14% off the cover price. It's quite a bargain. Shipping and handling is just 50¢ per book in the U.S. and 75¢ per book in Canada.* I understand that accepting the 2 free books and gifts places me under no obligation to buy anything. I can always return a shipment and cancel at any time. Even if I never buy another book, the two free books and gifts are mine to keep forever.

150/350 HDN FV42

Name	(PLEASE PRINT)	
Address		Apt. #
City	State/Prov.	Zip/Postal Code

Signature (if under 18, a parent or guardian must sign)

Mail to the **Harlequin® Reader Service:**
IN U.S.A.: P.O. Box 1867, Buffalo, NY 14240-1867
IN CANADA: P.O. Box 609, Fort Erie, Ontario L2A 5X3

Want to try two free books from another line?
Call 1-800-873-8635 or visit www.ReaderService.com.

* Terms and prices subject to change without notice. Prices do not include applicable taxes. Sales tax applicable in N.Y. Canadian residents will be charged applicable taxes. Offer not valid in Quebec. This offer is limited to one order per household. Not valid for current subscribers to Harlequin Blaze books. All orders subject to credit approval. Credit or debit balances in a customer's account(s) may be offset by any other outstanding balance owed by or to the customer. Please allow 4 to 6 weeks for delivery. Offer available while quantities last.

Your Privacy—The Harlequin® Reader Service is committed to protecting your privacy. Our Privacy Policy is available online at www.ReaderService.com or upon request from the Harlequin Reader Service.

We make a portion of our mailing list available to reputable third parties that offer products we believe may interest you. If you prefer that we not exchange your name with third parties, or if you wish to clarify or modify your communication preferences, please visit us at www.ReaderService.com/consumerschoice or write to us at Harlequin Reader Service Preference Service, P.O. Box 9062, Buffalo, NY 14269. Include your complete name and address.

HB13R

It was her. He knew it.

Eli Weston chuckled low, the sound rife with irony, then brought the bottle to his lips once again. Southern Comfort—appropriate, considering that was the only form of relief he was likely to get during this godforsaken week from hell. Water sloshed against the side of the tub and splashed onto the back porch as he deliberately shifted into a more relaxed position. It didn't matter that he was wound tighter than a two-dollar watch, that the mere thought of her sent a bolt of heat directly into his groin.

Perception, naturally, was key.

How did he know it was her who'd pulled into the driveway? The particular sound of her car door? The crunch of a light-footed person across the gravel? Those keen senses honed by years of specialized military training?

Ha. As if.

Nothing that sophisticated, unfortunately. It was the tightening of his gut, the prickling of his skin across the nape of his neck, the slight hesitation from the moment the car motor turned off until the driver decided to exit the vehicle. As though she was steeling herself, preparing to face him.

That was what had given her away.

"I'm back here," he called before she could mount the front porch steps.

She hesitated once again, then resumed movement and changed direction. Eli closed his eyes and prayed that she'd be in something other than that damned dress she'd had on earlier today. It was white, short and...flouncy. Not the least bit inappropriate, but somehow it managed to be sexy as hell all the same. It hugged her curvy frame, showcased her healthy tan and moved when she did. The hem fluttered just so with every swing of her hips, a silent "take me" with each step she took.

It was infuriatingly, unnervingly hot.

A startled "Oh" made him open his eyes, his gaze instinctively shifting toward the direction of the sound.

He mentally swore. Just his luck—she was still wearing it.

"There's a shower inside," she said tightly. "Could you get out of there? I need to talk to you."

He shrugged lazily, then stood. Water sloshed over the sides and sluiced down his body. He pushed his hair back from his face, careful to flex his biceps in the process.

He arched a deliberate brow. "Anything for you, sweetheart. Happy now?"

The last person Eli Weston can afford to be attracted to is the only woman he wants. Find out why by picking up THE RULE-BREAKER by Rhonda Nelson.

Available March 19.

A new installment in the bestselling Mighty Quinns series by Kate Hoffmann

When Jack Quinn's mother and Jenna McMahon's father hook up, the kids are not all right. But as Jenna and Jack work to keep their parents apart, they realize that family ties run deep, but passion and desire run even deeper.

Pick up

The Mighty Quinns: Jack

by *Kate Hoffmann*

AVAILABLE MARCH 19, 2013